Michael

when a catastrophe answers prayers

Kirk S. Jockell

D1714829

The Free Mullet Press, LLC

For Rhonda and Phil

1

The meteorologists at NHC, the National Hurricane Center, were counting down the days. The first of November was right around the corner and would mark the official end of the annual hurricane season. It was a day to celebrate and a good reason to breathe a little easier. While it's not totally unheard of, tropical weather events in November are quite rare. Hurricane Kate was the last late-season hurricane to make landfall on US soil, and it did so as a Category 2 storm on the Florida Panhandle. Life has been pretty well quiet since.

While November had not yet arrived, the season appeared to be slowing down. There was, however, one pesky tropical disturbance that held the team's casual attention.

"Hey, Ted. What's the latest on that new Central America system north of Panama?"

"Boring, Alan. Been watching it for a couple of days now. Lots of enhanced convection in a broad area of low pressure, but the wind shear is knocking its dick in the dirt. It's very disorganized and expected to move north soon with that incoming trough. Looks like a non-event, but we might want to consider designating it as a Potential Tropical Cyclone and put out an advisory, just in case." He looked up at his boss.

"Better to be safe than sorry, Alan."

"Agreed."

And they did. Later that afternoon, an advisory announcing Potential Tropical Cyclone Fourteen went out on the wire. It predicted a high-end tropical storm making landfall within a "Cone of Uncertainty" that stretched from New Orleans to Cedar Key. While the report went out and the local coastal news agency reported on it, it was noise to most people's ears. After all, who really pays attention to the news on a Saturday afternoon?

Over the course of the next day, despite a westerly wind shear of thirty-five miles per hour, the storm ignored all deteriorating influences and continued to develop. The storm's persistence could not be ignored. They upgraded it to a tropical depression, and within hours, Tropical Storm Michael was born.

The NHC immediately put out an advisory that the storm had achieved named status. They warned of landfall sometime Wednesday anywhere within the cone of uncertainty and that it *could* achieve hurricane status by Tuesday night or Wednesday.

During Sunday night, the storm strengthened more. Before daylight could hit the shores of the Gulf Coast, hurricane hunting aircraft were inside the storm recording sustained wind speeds in excess of 77 miles per hour. Not good.

Early the next morning, October 8th, the NHC and the southern coastal states woke up to Hurricane Michael. The storm now had the full attention of meteorologists, and the landfall cone had narrowed some. Michael was still predicted to make its final approach on October 10th, but where was still anybody's guess.

Later that morning, at the 10:00 am briefing, Alan sat at

the end of an enormous conference table along with others on the team. The meeting started on time when Ted took to the podium and fired up his PowerPoint presentation. He stood silent, looking at the latest image.

"Come on, Ted," said his boss. "Where the hell are we? I have a conference call with FEMA and the coastal governors at noon. Scott is especially concerned."

"I don't like it," said Ted. "I don't like it at all."

"What is it, dammit? Out with it!"

"It's a potential monster, Alan. It's going to be a real bastard."

"Ted, it was just upgraded to a Category 1 this morning."

"Yeah, but look," Ted started flipping through his slides. "Here you can see that the upper-level wind shear that had been slowing its progress is weakening. In short order, it will be non-existent."

His boss said nothing.

Ted hit the remote and a new slide appeared on the screen. "And look at the abundance of moisture in the upper atmosphere. With no shear, it's only going to get worse, especially when it hits the warmer waters of the upper Gulf of Mexico. The region just had an extremely hot September, with Florida breaking records statewide for the entire month." Ted took his pointer and circled a huge portion of the gulf. "This water is hot. Real hot, and it is going to add fuel to a fire."

"Direction?" asked Alan.

Ted jumped to another screen and used the laser pointer again. "Currently, this large ridge of high-pressure off the Eastern seaboard is nudging it toward the north-northwest, but..."

"But what?"

"It goes away, and..." He clicked for the next screen.

"Its directional influence will be replaced by this upper-level low-pressure trough coming down and across the continental US. It is a large system, and its southwesterly flow will steer Michael in a new direction. There will be nothing to stop or slow its intensification."

"What's the bottom-line?"

"The bottom-line is... Governor Scott has every reason to be concerned."

"What's your best prediction?"

Ted raised his hand, showed four fingers and a thumb, but said, "High-end Category 3." He wanted to say Cat 5 but didn't want to hear the words come out of his mouth.

His boss took the hint and thought, *Okay, if we don't come right out and say it, maybe it will never happen.*

Elsewhere, in central Florida, outside of Tampa, another weather enthusiast was watching the storm. He had been giving it more attention than those at the NHC, playing around and studying the various computer models and watching the surrounding weather systems that would ultimately drive it toward landfall. He didn't like it either. The elevated water temps in the upper Gulf of Mexico gave him exceptional concern. He knew what the three to five degree increase over the normal average meant, and there was nothing good about it. In the back of his mind, he had one thought. *Camille.*

He prepared his makeshift home studio. His adoring fans on Facebook were expecting him to go live at the top of the hour. He didn't want to be late. The page went live, and he shared his computer screen. As he waited for folks to join the session, he went to the bar and poured a long, stiff drink. He felt like he would need it for this session. After settling down in his chair, he positioned the microphone, looked into the camera, and said, "Hey, everybody. It's your Drunk Donkey here. Boy, do we have some things to go over. Tropical Storm Michael wasted no time. Folks, he's a hurricane now."

2

WILSON COUNTY, TN: MEMORIAL DAY 2011

The day was anything but quiet, but few Memorial Days are. The poor ladies working at the 911 dispatch center stayed busy for the better part of the day. Especially after the noon hour, when the celebratory beers, wines, whiskey, and weed ran free through the systems of those enjoying the holiday. They weren't alone. While the dispatch staff manages the lion's share of calls, they hand off the rest to sister agencies. On holidays, the police, deputies, firemen, paramedics, and EMTs run calls all day. In short, it sucked pulling duty on Memorial Day until the crazies and the keepers of shenanigans settled down to sleep it off.

Even though the first day of summer is in June, many view Memorial Day as the official start of the season. This might be fine in most locations, but when a significant body of water makes up your location, you can expect every boat in the area to be rushing to the boat ramps. For Wilson County, it is the Cumberland River. This means that besides members of local public safety, the Tennessee Wildlife Resource Agency and their patrol boats would be busy too. Booze and boats don't mix, but that's a message that doesn't seem to resonate with the, *I got this, hold my beer,* crowd.

It was a little after 8:30 in the evening when the inbound

calls slowed. By 9:00, they fell to a trickle, and the dispatch staff caught a well-deserved break.

Leading up to that point was *Amateur Hour*. Law enforcement ran calls to cover five different alcohol-involved accidents, one with a fatality. The fire department extinguished a fully involved house fire that originated from a turkey fryer explosion in a garage. Paramedics and EMTs were called to treat everything from minor cases of, *I've fallen, and I can't get up,* to several serious calls involving inebriation. They treated burns, luckily none too severe from the house fire, and later a self-inflicted knife wound as a result of cleaning fish under the influence. The med squad found a good laugh when they were called to multiple buttock burns. Several young men simultaneously launched quite sizable bottle rockets from the cheeks of their asses.

However, of the multiple calls on the river involving plenty of BUI arrests, there were three serious accidents. One guy ran his Bayliner cruiser up on the rocks, and another smashed into a private dock. The worst involved a cigarette boat running at full speed around a bank, striking a pontoon boat, killing three of the seven passengers and hospitalizing two others. One casualty was an eleven-year-old boy. Sad, tragic, and avoidable.

As the call center kept their fingers crossed and an eye on the switchboard, on the western side of the county in the town of Mount Juliet, a widow and her little dachshund were ending their day.

***

She emerged from her bedroom wearing nothing but an old, comfortable night shirt from Walmart or Target. She couldn't remember which. It was a favorite and showed many years of use, including gaping holes left from the teething habits of an overzealous puppy. After recharging her wine glass with what remained in the bottle, she went to the living room to enjoy the last cigarette of the day.

She sat on the sofa and grabbed the pack of Virginia Slims Menthol 120s that sat on the coffee table.

"Well, shit," she said to the dog. "It's empty."

The carton wasn't far. Problem solved.

After lighting her cigarette, she placed it in the ashtray's holder and sat back. Zoey, her dog, jumped up in her lap and provided kisses to her face.

"Oh, Zoey! Now knock it off."

Zoey did, then curled up in a ball within reach.

After a sip of wine, the woman reached for her cigarette and brought it to her lips. She looked at the burning end and wanted to put it down, but the fragrant menthol was more than she could resist. After all, she has been smoking since her teens. She loved it. Not uncommon for people from where she was raised. Everybody smoked, or so it seemed. It was only natural. She started with the Benson & Hedges Menthol 100s, but later graduated to the longer, more sexy and sophisticated Virginia Slims. However, lately, something had changed. She could feel it. And it scared her.

Over the last few months, the enjoyment had faded. Not because of the decreasing pleasure of the smoke, but because of the chest pains she knew awaited her once she went to bed. But while the enjoyment faded, the desire did not. After she filled her lungs and exhaled, she put the long stick back on the ashtray. An epiphany hit her. She wasn't in control. For decades, she thought she had been. But no.

"Oh my God," she said aloud. Then, after another sip of

wine, she closed her eyes to pray. "Lord of lords. Please help me. Take this *want* away from me. The thing that pulls at me. Take this addiction that controls my life. Take it away."

It was a profound moment. Never had she even considered stopping the cigarettes. The thought, while comforting, seemed impossible without divine intervention. She took another sip of wine.

On an end table sat a picture. She picked it up. The image held a big smile. Love radiated from the frame. It was from a happier time, a good party.

"I sure love and miss you. Why did you have to go so soon?"

The picture looked back and said nothing.

A box of tissues was nearby. *Poof. Poof.* She pulled two sheets and dried her tears.

She spoke to the face that looked back at her. "I know. I know. It's been years, but I just can't seem to move on. Help me, dammit."

She placed the picture on the sofa, memory up, so she could glance at it. After sipping the last of her wine, she closed her eyes.

It was an hour and a half later when her eyes opened, though she didn't realize it. Zoey was curled up, asleep in her lap. The empty wine glass was still in her hand and the cigarette had extinguished itself, burning into the filter.

After putting the picture back where it belonged and setting the glass next to the ashtray, she gathered up Zoey in her arms. "C'mon, baby. Let's go to bed."

Once comfortable, the weight of the world joined her, pressing her down through the mattress. It was like an elephant sitting on her chest. It had become a familiar feeling, but this time was worse. Zoey paced the mattress back and forth beside her. She tried to calm her pup, but then something grabbed her right arm like a tightening vise that wouldn't stop.

"Oh, dear!" she cried out.

She tried to remain still, hoping it would go away, but it would not relent, and the pain darted up into her neck like a spike. It was then she knew. She clutched at her chest and reached for her phone.

3

WILSON COUNTY MED UNIT 17

They had great hopes that the quiet they enjoyed in the 911 call center would continue. Many crossed their fingers tight, hoping for all the drunks to be passed out cold and safe somewhere. They prayed that the last of the dangerous drivers were now off the road and that the streets stayed quiet from trouble or violence. Not that the latter was ever much of a problem. Not in Wilson County, anyway.

One person said, "Do you think..."

"Don't say it!" said another. "You'll jinx us."

The quiet lasted a few minutes more. Right after one in the morning, the switchboard lit up.

Somebody said, "Well, shit! A good thing never lasts."

Expecting some party complaint or another elderly person looking for conversation, Kara, the next girl in the rotation, rolled her eyes as she answered the call. "Wilson County 911. What is your emergency?" The second she heard the voice on the other side of the line, Kara sat up straighter. "Repeat that, please."

The voice on the other line said, "I'm having a heart attack! I just know it. It hurts something awful. Oh, my God... help!"

"What is your name and what is your location?"

"My name is Charlene Jones and I'm at home in Mt. Juliet."

Charlene gave the dispatcher the address.

"I'm sending help immediately and I will remain on the line until the paramedics arrive. Try to stay calm and help me out a little. How old are you?"

"God, please hurry. I'm fifty. A white female." She wasn't sure why she added the last part, but it seemed appropriate.

"Thank you, Charlene. Take it easy. Where in the house are you?"

"I'm not in the house anymore. I'm in the front yard. My little dog is inside, and I don't want it to get.... OH! It hurts. Please hurry!"

She dropped her phone and lay curled up in the wet grass, trying to find any position that might bring comfort.

"Charlene? Charlene? Are you there?"

Another dispatcher asked, "Is she not there anymore?"

"She's there," said Kara. "I can hear her groaning. It's awful." Her words would fall on deaf ears, but Kara raised her voice to provide encouragement. "Charlene. Stay with me. Everything is going to be okay. Can you hear me?"

After several minutes, Kara looked up at the other dispatchers that had gathered around her booth. She held up a finger. "Yes. I hear the sirens. They're almost there." Focusing back on her caller. "Can you hear that, Charlene? Can you? Help is almost there. Just hang on."

***

The Wilson County Med Unit 17 approached the house with full lights and sirens. A nearby streetlamp provided illumination on the grass and the situation before them.

"What the hell do we have here?" asked the paramedic.

"She looks crazy as a loon," said the driver and EMT. "I bet she's just drunk."

They parked on the curb and got out. They were swift with their actions. The EMT grabbed a couple boxes of gear, while the paramedic remained calm but hurried in his approach toward the near-naked woman lying in the grass, crawling in circles on her side, her nightshirt piled up around her neck, and her purse thrown to the side, contents spilled on the grass.

The paramedic kneeled next to her and stopped her movements. "Hello, Ma'am. Can you hear me?"

His patient nodded her head.

"Will you open your eyes and look at me?"

She did, and the terrified look she returned tightened his sphincter and sense of urgency. She was pale and sweating profusely.

"What is your name, ma'am?"

"Charlene!" She clutched at her chest. "Ohhhh! It hurts. Charlene Jones."

"Hello Charlene, I'm Jonathan Cannon. I'm a paramedic." He pointed at his partner. "And that is Mark Chester. He's an EMT. We are here to help." Cannon looked at Chester and said, "Get the stretcher. We need to get her in the truck. Pronto."

The EMT turned to run.

"Ms. Jones, how old are you?"

"Fifty!"

"Are you allergic to anything? Any meds or what have you?"

She didn't answer and continued to clutch her chest.

He asked again and still nothing.

"Charlene! This is important! Are you allergic to any medications? Answer me!"

She responded with a shake of her head and whimpered,

"No."

"One more question. Are you on, or have you taken any medications tonight?"

She answered with a violent shake of her head.

"Very good. Thank you. Sorry I yelled. Here comes Chester with the stretcher."

She repeated his words with a very brief smile. "Chester and the stretcher."

Her sense of humor gave Cannon hope, but that comfort fled his mind as she bowed her back and bellowed with pain. "Pleeeeease help me!"

Once they got her in the truck, they went to work. She couldn't lay still. The pain wouldn't allow it.

"Ms. Jones? Look at me."

She did.

"We need to put in an IV line. You are going to have to be still for us." Cannon looked at his EMT. "Large bore. You find a good vein. I'll try to keep her calm."

"Look at me, Ms. Jones."

She did.

"Easy now. Try to stay calm." He rubbed her head, smiled, and they maintained eye contact. "I know it hurts. Try to think of something happy."

She said, "Zoey."

He smiled at her. "Okay. Zoey it is. Who is Zoey?"

"My little dog."

From behind Cannon, Chester announced, "We're in!"

"Very good, Ms. Jones. You did really good. Chester is going to check your blood pressure now." Canon continued to work as he spoke. "I'm hooking you up to my cardiac monitor. You know an EKG. You know what that is, right? I need to see what is going on in there."

As Cannon finished connecting the twelve-lead EKG to his patient, Chester said, "One thirty-two over eighty-four."

"One thirty-two over eight-four. Copy that, Mark."

Canon finished up by adding the defibrillation pads, just in case. Then he turned on the unit and monitored the electro-activity of her heart. He didn't like what he was looking at, so turned to Chester and said, "I'll finish up. Get us to Tristar Summit. Pronto."

Cannon put on a fake smile. "Ms. Jones. Can you chew and swallow for me?"

She nodded with a grimace. "I think so."

Cannon produced four chewable aspirins and a cup of water. "Open your mouth."

She did, and he placed the tablets on her tongue. "Chew these up for me." After watching her swallow, he held her head up so she could take some water.

After she confirmed with a nod of her head, he felt the ambulance surge forward, and he rifled through his bag until he found the bottle of nitro. "Ms. Jones. This is a sublingual med. It is nitroglycerin. Don't chew it or swallow it. Let it dissolve under your tongue. Okay?"

She didn't hesitate to open her mouth and lift her tongue.

"Very good. Just let it dissolve. It should help a little bit."

Then he prepared a dose of blood-thinning Heparin and injected it into the IV port.

As Med Unit 17 bounced down the road, he spoke to his patient. "How are we doing, Ms. Jones? Are you still with me? How is the pain?"

She answered with a grunt.

Then he grabbed the radio. "Tristar Summit. Tristar Summit. This is Wilson County Med Unit 17. Come in."

"Go ahead, Wilson County."

Cannon's spirits were lifted when he recognized the voice. "Doc Conrad. Is that you?"

"Yeah, Jonathan. It's me..."

"Good, because..."

"And listen, Johnny. We're done with drunks tonight. Just find them a park bench or something."

"No drunk, Doc. I have a white, fifty-year-old female suffering from severe chest pain. We are en route. She is pale with profuse sweat. Alert and responsive. Pupils are equal and reactive to light. BP was one thirty-two over eighty-four. After 324 milligrams of aspirin, nitro, and heparin, it has come down a little. One twenty-eight over eighty. I have the twelve-lead monitor running. I don't like it, Doc."

"What are you seeing, Johnny?"

"Tombstones, Doc. Elevated ST segments with T waves rubbing the ceiling."

"What's your ETA?"

Chester had been listening to the transmission and yelled back to Cannon. "Six mikes."

"Did you hear that, Doc? About six minutes."

Dr. Conrad found the nearest nurse and asked, "Who is the cardiologist on duty tonight?"

"Dr. Green, sir."

"Find him and let him know he's needed down here in less than four."

Dr. Conrad spoke into the mike. "Roger that on the six. Make it five."

Cannon hung up the radio and felt the med unit surge forward. "Get us there in one piece, Mark."

As Cannon monitored her vitals and heart activity, she groaned and grunted with pain. The waves of discomfort were increasing in frequency. "Please," she said. "It hurts so terribly bad."

He wanted to give as few meds as possible pre-hospital, but her next bellowing caused an extreme strain on her heart and system. He prepared and injected three milligrams of morphine into her IV port. That worked quickly and took off the edge.

Jonathan Cannon was laser focused on the cardiac monitor, watching every detail. His patient seemed to be resting and still. The ride to the hospital seemed to last forever. It always does when life is in balance and the same life is in your hands.

He called over his shoulder to Chester. "How are we doing, dammit?"

"Four minutes."

"Son of a bitch! It was six just ten minutes ago."

"Doing the best I can, brother."

From the head of the stretcher, he heard her say, "What is your name again?"

"Jonathon, ma'am. Jonathan Cannon."

She reached with one hand and squeezed his arm. "Can I call you Johnny?"

"Yes, ma'am. That would be fine."

"Please, call me Charlene. How old are you, Johnny?"

"Thirty, ma'am... I mean, Charlene."

With the first genuine smile he'd seen on her face, she asked, "Are you married?"

"Yes. Fourteen years this September."

She gave a little cough, closed her eyes, and uttered, "Lucky girl."

Cannon didn't know why, but he didn't like how the conversation was going. And he didn't like that she became quiet and closed her eyes. "Charlene. Stay with me now. Open your eyes. No time for a nap. We are almost there.

Charlene! Wake up!" Then the warning lights flashed on the screen. "Shit!" He turned his head. "Chester! She's going into V-Tach!"

"Less than two."

Three seconds later, a pain overcame her that the morphine could not keep at bay. She clutched at her chest, raised her head, and called out. "It hurts! I'm dying!"

Cannon looked at her and, as she fell unconscious, said, "Not in my truck! Dammit! ... Chester!"

"Almost there! I see the parking lot."

"Hurry! Dialing up 200 joules now." As he waited for the charge to complete, he said, "Come on, Charlene. Don't do this to me. Not tonight. Ride the lightning and make it good."

He felt the turn and familiar hope of the curb. They were there. He wasted no time and hit her with the paddles. She violently came up off the stretcher and flopped back. Cannon looked at the monitor. The electrical activity that had once been there was now gone. "Shit!" Her airway was still clear, so he bagged her a couple of times to get fresh oxygen in her lungs. Then he jumped to chest compressions, near impossible to do properly in a moving ambulance, but necessary.

He heard the beeping and felt the truck backing up to the door and within seconds the back door of the med unit flew open. Cannon turned his head toward the lighted entrance and saw Dr. Conrad.

"Where are we, Johnny?"

"Code four. Full cardiac and respiratory arrest."

"How long?"

"Less than a minute."

Dr. Conrad found the nurse with the clipboard. "Mark the time, Kristen... Okay folks," he said, addressing the rest of the emergency room staff. "Let's go. We got work to do. Get her inside."

Cannon did his best to continue the chest compressions as they backed the stretcher out, dropped the legs, and rolled her into the emergency room door. A staff member took over for Cannon. Another nurse took over bagging the airway and commented, "Very clammy and gray, Doc."

"Clammy and gray. Got it. Thank you." He turned back to Cannon. "Any meds other than what we discussed on the radio?" asked Dr. Conrad.

"No."

"So, no epi or atropine?"

"Negative. No time."

"Very good. Thanks."

They rushed her down the hall. Green, the cardiologist, met them outside critical care bay one. "Well, what do you have for me, Patrick?"

"Nothing yet, Steve. Step aside and let us do our thing."

As they rolled her into the bay, Dr. Green said, "You woke me up, you know."

Conrad stopped, winked, pumped his bushy eyebrows, and said, "I'll make it worth your while. Then you can go back to watching your porn. Take a seat. This shouldn't take too long." Then he slung the curtain closed.

Before the med unit and Charlene Jones rolled in, the emergency room staff, much like the 911 call center, had been hoping the rest of the evening would stay quiet. It had already been a long day, treating both trauma and shenanigans. Everyone was exhausted. And had Charlene been an eighty-seven-year-old woman, they would have still responded the same. The expectations, however, would have been different. But that wasn't the case. Charlene was young. She had a fighting chance. They just had to get her back. And that fact alone had every staff member's adrenaline flowing like expresso coffee. It was showtime!

Inside, Conrad stood at the head of the bed and intubated his patient while giving orders. His team knew him well enough that they acted in anticipation of his every instruction. "One milligram epi, stat, and fifty milli equivalents of sodium bicarb. Start a new line in the other arm. Foley catheter, please. Let's get a tube in her stomach. Kristen? How are we doing on time?"

"A little over two minutes, sir."

He watched as they injected the epinephrine into the IV port. Many times, that's all it takes to get things moving again. Not this time. *Damn*, he thought. He looked at the nurse handling the meds. "Let's go with a milligram of atropine."

She stood ready with the syringe. Just waiting for the order.

And that is how it went for several minutes. Chest compressions, bagging the airway, more epi, more atropine. Things were not looking good.

4

CHICAGO, IL: MEMORIAL DAY 2011

B ill looked at his watch. It was a little after 8 a.m. The
workday for the office in Maharashtra, India, would
wrap up soon, so it should be anytime now. He came in
especially early in case the report arrived ahead of schedule,
but no luck. That was okay with him. After pouring another
cup of Earl Grey tea, he kicked his feet up and gazed out
his twenty-third-floor office window toward the horizon. The
calm waters of Lake Michigan were in between. The Windy
City wasn't living up to its name. Except for the occasional
zephyr that tickled the surface, the lake was a mill pond for as
far as the eyes could see. *Beautiful*, he thought.

His eyes trailed back toward shore and over the Monroe
Harbor mooring field that serves as the seasonal home to
several hundred boats. Mostly sailboats. The idea of a boating
life was foreign to him, but it seemed appealing. Not in
Chicago, though.

"Christ," he'd say. "What a pain in the ass it must be!"

And it's true, the boating season on Lake Michigan is only
six months long. May through October. By November, the
boats below would have to be pulled and put into dry storage
for the winter months. The icing over of the harbor would
be just around the corner. No, he liked the idea of something

warmer.

A slight grimace stretched across his face as he gazed around at the rest of the city. The idea of staying and working in such an environment wore his spirit down. The crowds, the crime, the noise, the people, and the hustle and bustle no longer held his attention. Not that it ever did. Chicago was where his career had led him. The job was there. Nothing more.

Ding!

A notification on his phone told him a new email awaited his attention.

He dropped his feet to the floor and turned his attention to his computer. India was calling. Twenty-three minutes behind schedule, but he didn't care. These things take time, and the contents of the data were all that mattered.

He finished his tea and pored over and analyzed the data sheets displayed on his computer screen. It was all good news for their client. The numbers were impressive, so the client would be happy and proud. The stockholders too. He constructed the final, smooth report that would go to the client. He couldn't wait to share the news.

Ding!

Another notification from his phone. This time a text message from Samantha, his girlfriend. He read it.

How long are you going to be?

He rolled his eyes. *As long as it takes.*

But it's Memorial Day!

Not in Leipzig, Germany.

The quarterly data that had come in was for Edeka, one of the largest and fastest-growing supermarket chains in Germany. Many projected that in the years to come, the store would take the top spot and enjoy as much as 20% or more of the market share. The report that Bill was trying to prepare would certainly help support that prognostication.

Can you not get one of the other guys to handle this?

She tested his patience. *There is nobody here but me. Everyone else is off for the holiday.*

Everybody but you. And you're the boss.

And it's not my bloody holiday, now is it?

He waited and looked at the screen, anticipating a reply. It didn't come. He closed his eyes and tried to remember his last thought before being interrupted. "Ah, yes," he said as his fingers addressed the keyboard.

Ding!

He rubbed and massaged his hairless head. "Bloody hell!"

He looked at the message. *Hurry! I want to go to the pool.*

He didn't reply and returned to work.

***

Had it not been at the insistence of his mum, Bill would have happily stayed in northern England and helped on the family farm. He loved the idea of being a farmer. It was hard work, but when you put forth the effort, the benefits are truly satisfying. The farm was nothing like the mega agribusiness operations found in the United States. It was a humble working farm, and Bill's father had put everything he had into it. They had little money, but they were *farm rich*.

When the time came, Bill's mum shipped him off to boarding school for an education and a different life path. He did well, but he hated it. The call of the farm pulled at him. He missed it so and took every opportunity to return home, even through college, to help his father. Between school, his studies, and the farm, there wasn't much time for anything else, including social outings and chasing skirts. That never bothered Bill, and it left him with an unparalleled work ethic that drove him toward success. Though his days as a farmer were numbered, he came to understand that Mum was right.

He studied mechanical engineering at university until an option to shift his focus to something more unusual caught his eye: biomedical engineering. He continued with his graduate degree, and ultimately, a PhD in orthopedics studies. When an opportunity arrived for him to run the facility at the research center of Sir John Charnley, the father of joint replacement, he jumped on it. That launched a successful career in biomedical research and development, which ultimately brought him to the United States.

Over the years, a new passion for information technology emerged. Specifically, data management and analytics. Ultimately, a professional shift took place and once again his work ethic and drive propelled him toward even greater success. He created a company and put together a top-notch team that now serves the analytical needs of some of the largest companies in the world.

***

After finishing the polished report, he encrypted and password-protected the file. Then he sent it on its merry way to Germany. Moments later... *Ding!* He looked at the screen, saw the familiar phone number, and replied with the password: *greatnumbers.*

Bill sat back in his chair and took in the lake view and the boats below. The wind had filled in, and several boats were leaving their moorings for a holiday cruise. The idea of a boating life re-entered his mind. He looked around the office. *Why do I need to be here?*

He answered himself aloud. "You don't. You can do what you do from anywhere." Then he leaned back and closed his eyes.

5

THE REUNION

When Charlene's eyes opened, she was in a dimly lit, foggy space with limited visibility. "Hello," she said. "Hello. What's going on?"

"Everything is fine," I said. "Scary, I know, but fine."

As I approached her through the haze, my features took shape, and she squinted her eyes in curiosity. When I came into clear focus, her eyes widened, and she said, "Michael?"

I smiled. "Yes, Charlie, it's me."

"Michael? My Michael? How can that be?"

I opened my arms, and she ran into my embrace.

6

MICHAEL JONES 07/06/1959–12/06/2004

O kay. I need to stop this story like scratching a needle across a Bobby Sherman album. It's time I get your attention, provide some background, and come clean.

I'm not just some voice coming off these pages, telling you some story, making it up as I go along. No... I have personal knowledge of the goings-on here. I've had a front-row seat to it all. I've even been instrumental in helping to shape some events to come.

In short... I'm Charlene's late husband, Michael Jones. Her friends call her Charlene, the grandkids call her Nay Nay, but she's always been Charlie to me.

Charlie isn't from Tennessee. She's from a tiny farm town called Iron City in the southwestern farm region of Georgia. The burbs of metropolitan Donalsonville and its grand population of twenty-eight hundred and twenty-two.

This is where we met, and over the years, we both have had our fair share of difficulties finding a soulmate, but my search ended when I met her. I'm not sure what she saw in me other than a fun time and my willingness to be true to her. I guess that was enough. She was my everything, and I'd like to think she felt the same about me. Alright... I know she did. If she didn't, she wouldn't continue to wear the ring I slipped on her finger the day we got hitched.

Oh, we had a great time together. It was pedal-to-the-metal: fun, love, and good times. A lot of good times. Whoo! Hoo! We were wide open, making the best of the time we had together. We enjoyed life so much that we couldn't stop laughing. And, if hard times pushed her to tears, I held her tight until it all passed. We loved each other so much.

Charlie and I had no regrets. Well... maybe that isn't altogether true. My only regret is that I left the party too soon. The party... huh! It was the party that caught up with me, and my liver couldn't stand the pace. Had I known there was a problem, perhaps I could have done something about it. But to be honest, probably not. Besides the steady and fun abuse of alcohol, I suffered from a severe case of Dupuytren's disease. It's an affliction that causes contractional deformities of the fingers and hands. For most, it isn't painful. I wasn't so lucky. The booze helped, but the addiction was worse. It's just how alcohol works with some people. I know that now.

Anyway, after sixteen months of a wonderful, happy marriage, I passed away, made her a widow, and left her with an old fixer upper and a mortgage. It killed me—pardon the pun—to leave, but in the end, it was best. My pain is gone.

Before Charlie, I got along okay. Sure, I hurt most days, but my life was fine. It just wasn't special. She changed all that. When I became sick, I never wanted to *live* so badly in my life. I didn't want *us* to end. In a way, *we* didn't.

I've been secretly watching over her ever since. So, while I was out of her life, she has remained in my... afterlife.

Charlie took my passing badly, very badly, and the mourning and sadness continued for years. She found it difficult to function, and it pained me to watch her endure it. She enjoyed some periods of happiness. I like to think I had something to do with that.

When she was asleep, I would often come to her and plant little seeds and ideas to keep her busy and active. Like the candy and gourmet gift store, she opened after my passing. Yup, my idea, and it did the trick for a couple of years. But her heart was no longer in Donalsonville. It was four hundred fifty-one miles north, in Tennessee with her daughter Madelyn and granddaughter, Ophelia. The frequent visits back and forth no longer satisfied Charlie's need to watch Ophelia grow up. She feared she would miss it all, so she loaded up the truck and she moved to Tennessee.

She moved to Mt. Juliet and found work in a women's boutique. Madelyn and Ophelia were about forty-five minutes away in Cookeville. It was a comfortable distance. Charlie was close enough and, at the same time, not under the feet of Madelyn and Spencer, her significant other.

Life in Tennessee was grand until that dreadful Memorial Day in 2011.

Okay, hopefully, that helps fill in some gaps for you folks. But before I continue with the story, here is a little advice. Be sincere. Thank God every day (He likes it when you do). Be kind to others. Don't be afraid to cry when your heart is warm. Take nothing for granted. Live your best life on Earth. And never... and I mean never, miss an opportunity to overuse the words, *I love you*.

There! I said it. I'll jump off my soapbox now.

7

THE REUNION... CONTINUED

She trembled. "Oh my God, Michael. I... I can't believe this. I have missed you so."

"I've missed you too, Charlie."

"Charlie ..." She smiled. "It's been so long since I've been called that. You were the only one."

"Kiss me, lady. We don't have a lot of time."

We kissed like we used to. Long, sweet, and passionate. When our lips parted, she cried.

"I don't understand," she said. "What is going on? You passed away. You left me."

I nodded my head. "Yes. I did, but I've never left you. I've been around all along."

She said nothing.

"Charlie, tell me. What do you last remember?"

She grabbed my neck for another hug. "I don't know. What does it matter? We're together now."

I had to push her away to look into her eyes. "Charlie. It's important. Think."

I watched as her eyes looked away to concentrate, then her eyes snapped back toward mine.

"I was in an ambulance. I had a heart attack." She was silent for a few beats, trying to piece everything together. Then her eyes grew wider, and she covered her mouth with her fingers. "Oh, no. I died."

"Sort of," I said.

"Oh my God! Zoey! Where's my Zoey?"

"Calm down, Charlie. Easy now. Zoey is fine. Trust me."

"Are you sure? How do you know?"

"I just do. You'll just have to believe me."

"I love you, Michael. I've never stopped loving you. Couldn't stop, even if I wanted to."

"I know. I have that effect on women."

She slapped my arm and laughed. It felt wonderful to hear that southern giggle again.

"Help me understand," she said. "What is this place?"

"A holding room of sorts."

"What am I doing here? Why are we here?"

I laughed.

"What's so funny?"

I pranced around, pretending to hold a cigarette between the ends of my fingers. "Oh, Dahl'n. You wouldn't have a little fire, would you? I seem to have misplaced my lighter."

Lucky for me, she was a good sport and laughed and slapped at me again.

"Oh, Michael. Knock it off."

I kept laughing. "You and your skinny cigarettes. I've never known anybody that loved their little habit more than you. The way you would lick your lips, bring that filter to your mouth and close your eyes to inhale. It left me feeling jealous."

"Just quit!" she said. "You hear me now?"

"I'm serious. You had an abnormal, sensuous love affair with every cigarette you ever knew."

"Had?"

"Yep. Prayers answered."

She gave me an odd stare.

"Don't you remember, silly? You asked God to 'take that *want* away.' Remember?"

"I guess, but it doesn't matter anymore." She ran in for another hug. "We're together again."

I hugged her back, and sadness came over me. After a while, I said, "Charlie. You can't stay."

She broke her hold and stepped back. "What do you mean? I don't understand."

"You got to go back. You're not ready for this." Then I laughed, and said, "Or this place isn't ready for you. I'm not sure which."

"Go where? I don't want to lose you again."

"Tennessee, and you won't lose me. I'll always be there, but... you must go back."

"This isn't fair. I just got here."

"I'm sorry, Charlie. I don't write the rules, but I'll be here when you return. Promise."

She said nothing.

"I love you, Charlie."

"How much time do we have left?"

"Not long, so kiss me before they bring you back."

"At least I'll have all this to take back with me."

We closed our eyes and dove into that last kiss. It was deep and loving, better than any first kiss ever felt. I held her tighter, not wanting her to go. It felt good to hold her again. We were so happy, but I couldn't bring myself to tell her she wouldn't remember any of this. Then... she was gone. Out of my arms. I smiled and cried.

***

"Kristen? Where are we?"

"Over ten minutes."

"Another five milligrams of epi, please."

He watched the nurse administer the dose and uttered, "Come on, lady. Not tonight. Not here."

And nothing happened. It was frustrating to everyone, including the guy doing the chest compressions. He was new to the staff. Finally, he stopped, balled up his fist, and hammered down on her chest as hard as he could. Nothing.

Everybody looked at him. They understood how he felt. They also knew his desperate effort was futile. They all looked at the cardiac monitor and the flat lines that stretched across the screen. Hopelessness seeped into their enthusiasm.

Then... there was a beep. Everyone's eyebrows lifted. Then there was another and another. Then the monitor danced as her heart jumped back into ventricular tachycardia.

Dr. Conrad said, "Well, what do you know, kids? We're back in the game. Hot damn! Dial up those joules and get ready to fly."

A few seconds later, he yelled, "CLEAR!"

8

THE RESURRECTION

It was the next day, in the early evening. As the nurse changed out an IV bag, she noticed Charlene stir. After calculating the proper drip count, she grabbed Charlene's hand and felt a squeeze. She immediately reached for the nurse call button and pressed it. A few moments later, a voice returned through the speaker. "Yes. How can I help you?"

"Sally. It's me, Cindy. She is coming around. Let Dr. Conrad know, ASAP."

"Will do."

Several minutes later, the first thing Charlene saw after regaining focus was the bright eyes and smile of a stranger. She turned her head and looked around the room. Others stood around her. Feeling dazed and confused, she said nothing as she returned her gaze to the stranger.

"Well... hello, Ms. Jones," said a man. "Welcome back."

His words meant nothing to her.

"I am Dr. Conrad. You and I met when you first arrived here. I've had the pleasure of having you under my care. You are safe and doing quite well, considering the circumstances."

Her voice cracked when she asked, "Where am I?"

"The ICU of TriStar Summit Medical Center. You suffered a severe heart attack."

She looked away to think, then gave the doctor a look of panic.

"Easy, now. You've been through quite an ordeal. The surgery went well..."

"Surgery?" Her voice cracked.

"Yes. Three stints. You are probably the luckiest lady in all of Wilson County right now. More on that at another time. I want you to rest. I'll be back to see you a bit later." He looked at the nurse in charge and said, "Contact me if there is any change."

Nurse Cindy approached Charlene and asked, "How are you feeling, Ms. Jones? Any nausea?"

She shook her head.

"That's good. Sometimes the anesthesia can leave you a little queasy."

"I'm thirsty." It hurt to talk.

"No liquids for another hour." She produced a cup. "But here are some ice chips to suck on. Go slow though."

Charlene waved the nurse closer. When she was close enough, she whispered, "My dog? Zoey?"

Nurse Cindy smiled. "Your sister said that would be the first thing you would ask about. The dog is fine."

"She's here?"

"And your daughter. The ER found their contact information in your purse. They've been worried sick. Once you have settled in, we can allow them back for a quick visit. We usually only allow one visitor at a time... but given the circumstances."

Charlene scrunched her eyes and nodded. "I would like that. Thank you."

"So, do you remember much of anything? Like calling 911?"

Charlene looked away to think and shook her head no.

"Don't worry. You're still groggy. I'm sure it will all come back to you." The nurse smiled. "Right now, though, you just lie back and rest. I'll be back in a bit to check on you."

Then she was alone in the big, strange room. She looked at all the tubes in her arms and the wires that flowed out from underneath her gown. She wondered if it was all a dream, but it wasn't. That much she knew, and the reality of the situation brought on a steady flow of tears. She closed her eyes and wept until she heard my voice.

"Stop your crying, Charlene."

She opened her eyes and looked around. "Huh?" She was still alone, but she did as she was told, then slipped off to sleep.

***

Her sister and daughter stood on either side of the bed. They each held one of her hands, gently squeezing. Charlene woke up and turned her head on her pillow from side to side to look at them. She stopped on her daughter and smiled.

"Hey, Mom," said Madelyn. "How do you feel?"

Charlene shrugged her shoulders, then turned to look at her sister, Jolene, and whispered, "Zoey?"

Jolene and Madelyn looked at each other and smirked.

"Huh! She's going to be just fine," said Jolene.

Madelyn said, "Momma... stop worrying about Zoey. She's okay. Breath is bad as ever."

That made Charlene smile.

"That was one hell of a scare you put into us," said Jolene.

"Water?"

"Yes," said Madelyn as she reached for the pitcher to pour a glass. "The nurse said you could have some now, but to take it easy."

Jolene pressed the button to raise the head of the bed, and Charlene took the glass. The water was room temperature, but it felt good against her throat. She came up for air, then went for another drink.

"Easy, dammit," said Madelyn.

Charlene nodded, set the glass down, and whispered, "I feel like I've been run over by a truck."

"Do you remember what happened?" asked Jolene.

She reached for her water and took another sip. "I remember lying in the yard hurting like hell. Oh, my goodness. I've never felt such pain."

"So, you do remember calling 911?" asked Madelyn.

She stopped to think. "Yeah. I had gone to bed..."

Charlene explained what had happened that night. Everything. She didn't miss a detail.

"What is the last thing you remember?" asked Jolene.

"I don't know. Riding in the ambulance to the hospital, I guess. Oh, how it hurt. I seem to remember one last bout of excruciating pain, then..." She tried to search for more, but nothing. "I don't know after that. It all goes dark."

Jolene and Madelyn exchanged worried looks.

"What?" asked Charlene. "What is it?"

Her daughter and sister continued to look at each other.

"What is it, dammit? What are you not telling me?"

"Well, it would seem that someone is feeling better."

All three ladies looked toward the door. Dr. Conrad had returned.

"Doc, they're not telling me something. I just know it. Exactly what in the world is going on?"

Now it was the doctor, Madelyn, and Jolene, who were looking at each other.

"Doctor?"

The good doctor looked at his patient and said, "Ms. Jones. May I call you Charlene?"

"Absolutely."

"Then please, call me Patrick."

"What's going on, Patrick?"

"Patience, Charlene. I'll tell you, but first tell me this. How much of what happened to you do you remember?"

Charlene's eyes left Dr. Conrad and scanned those of her daughter and sister. Then she focused on the good doctor. "Patrick, why is everybody so *damn* interested in what I remember?"

"Because you were dead, Momma! You were gone. Dr. Patrick saved your life."

"Now. Now. Now," said the doctor. "It wasn't just me. It was a team effort."

Charlene said nothing.

Dr. Conrad sat on the edge of the bed and took Charlene's hand. "Charlene, I'm not used to fifty-year-old women coming into my ER dead and later holding my hand."

"I don't understand."

Madelyn said, "Momma, you..."

Dr. Conrad raised his hand toward Madelyn. "Please. Let's be a little more delicate."

Charlene said, "Don't mind her, Patrick. She's never been one to hold back. She calls 'em like she sees 'em." Then she smiled and looked at her daughter. "She comes by it honestly." After a beat or two, she continued, "Now, what is this all about?" She gave the doctor her undivided attention.

"When we first met, you had already passed on. The paramedics said that you flatlined as they rolled into the parking lot. When I got to you, you were unresponsive, and your breathing had stopped. We immediately took you into a room and went to work. My team is excellent, collectively they are much more talented than me.

"We were all exhausted and getting a rest and breather from a busy day of handling all the other holiday injuries and cases of party nonsense. However, there was something different about how you interrupted our very abbreviated period of relaxation. Your death gave us renewed energy and life to fight. Failure wasn't an option, and we got you back."

Charlene said nothing.

"I can promise. Had you been just another gash in the head from a broken beer bottle, you'd still be sitting in the ER lounge waiting on the next shift to come in."

"How long was I... gone?"

Again, the doctor and girls exchanged glances.

"A little over ten minutes."

Charlene gasped.

"You entered a state of Cerebral Hypoxia. Lack of oxygen to the brain. At about four to five minutes, brain cells die at an alarming rate. After ten minutes... Well, there's no sense even talking about that now, is there?"

"That's why we were asking the questions," said Jolene. "Brain damage, you know."

"And how did she do?" asked the doctor of the ladies.

"She seems to remember everything."

"Well, that is certainly good news, but we will still need a neurologist to examine her, just to be sure."

"Momma, who is the governor of Georgia?"

She smiled, "Nathan Deal."

Jolene asked, "Who is the president of the United States?"

Charlene rolled her eyes and grunted, "Obama."

Madelyn said, "She's fine."

Charlene and the doctor were still holding hands. She squeezed hard. "Thank you. For everything."

He squeezed back, let her go, and stood. "No, thank you for not ruining our night."

"By the way," Charlene said, "Was it you that did the surgery?"

"Ha!" The doctor laughed. "And what... ruin my good work in the ER? I think not. That would have been Dr. Green. He's an excellent cardiologist. I'm sure he will be by when he makes his rounds."

After more thanks from Charlene, Madelyn, and Jolene, the doctor excused himself. "Ladies, I've got to get back to the ER. Charlene, do you mind if I check in on you from time to time?"

"That would be nice."

"And one other thing, Ms. Charlene."

She said nothing.

"You are quite fortunate to have this new lease on life, but I can assure you of this... if you continue to smoke, you *will* be back in here within five years. I can promise you that. And chances are your outcome won't be so desirable."

She would never touch another cigarette. It amazed her how quickly she came to hold a vicious disdain for the things. The mere idea of placing one in her mouth made her sick. And from time to time, she could hear the words of the doctor repeated in her mind. And she always replied like she did the first time in the hospital. "You don't have to tell me twice."

Dr. Conrad tugged at an imaginary hat and slipped out the door.

"Momma! He's nice and handsome."

Jolene added, "And no wedding ring."

"Y'all hush up with that goofy talk."

"I'm jus say'n, Momma."

Charlene bit her lip and said, "He is kind of cute, huh?"

The three of them shared a laugh that felt good.

Madelyn took up a position on the edge of the bed and said, "So, Momma, what did you see?"

"What do you mean?"

"On the other side. Did you see anything? You know. The bright light or something."

Jolene said, "Or were you floating, looking down on your body as they worked on you?"

Charlene looked down to remember. She did this for a while before raising her head with a distraught look on her face. "Nothing. I don't remember seeing a thing." She looked at her daughter. "Oh my God. Nothing. What does that mean?"

9

CHICAGO, IL: WINTER 2012

B ill stood alone in his office, looking out the window over Lake Michigan. Though, is it really a lake after it freezes? A glacier perhaps. Yes, that is more like it.

Regardless, winters in Chicago suck. The freezing temperatures, wind, chill factor, all make for miserable conditions. To add insult to injury, there is the dreaded lake effect snow. The lake doesn't completely freeze over, so strong, icy winds from the north gather moisture from the warmer waters of the lake to relocate it on shore as a mighty white nuisance. Even the most moderate winter season takes its toll on any rational human being. Bill Salisbury was one such person. He hated the Chicago winters, and that day, he said aloud, "Enough. I've bloody had it."

The idea of buying a boat and heading toward warmer climates remained in the back of his head. Again, if he had an Internet signal, he could run his company from anywhere. It was a challenge he was ready to take on. And while he could afford any boat that would satisfy his needs, there was another challenge that picked at his technological mind.

Bill had become fascinated with the idea of living off the grid. He enjoyed and devoured all the YouTube channels and videos of folks that sought a life removed from the dependency of the outside world. He thought, *What if I applied that to a boat? An off-grid vessel that could sustain itself away from outside influences. Wouldn't that be something?*

The more he pondered on the idea, the more excited he got. He spun away from the window and said, "Bloody hell. Yes!"

He sat at his desk, grabbed a pad of paper and pen, and brainstormed. *What would I want in such a boat?*

The pen hit the page, and a list appeared.

~No internal combustion engine (electric propulsion)
~Solar Panels (how many???)
~Batteries (many batteries, must be lithium)
~Inverter (must be able to convert DC to AC for appliances)
~Water maker (must be able to make fresh H2O)
~Air Conditioning (<u>More Batteries!</u> Must handle load.)

He looked at the list and smiled. It was a good start. He didn't worry about all the technical details of how it would all come together. Those things he would research and nail down later. While he would never admit it or boast, Bill had a brilliant mind. It would be a fun puzzle for him. He liked that kind of work.

As he gazed over his list, he quickly realized something was missing. "Shit. I need a boat." Then he added it to the list.

The idea of electric propulsion has been around for a very long time. All you must do is look back at the days before the US Navy launched the USS Nautilus (SSN-571), the world's first nuclear submarine. Before then, all US subs were propelled by huge electric motors and charged by diesel engines while on the surface or just below the surface using a snorkel. Diesel-electric submarines are still in operational service all around the world.

Now, this isn't meant to be a history lesson, only to show that the idea isn't new. It's just that in 2012, the idea hadn't resurfaced in the production of pleasure yachts. Bill knew this would be a project boat. Another challenge he was willing to accept. All he needed was a sound boat to implement his plan.

After an extensive search, he found a 45-foot Carver that sat on-the-hard off the western shore of Lake Michigan in Wisconsin. The engines were shot, and the owner was looking to make a deal.

In the spring of 2013, Bill drove up to see the boat. The broker met Bill at the yard, then leaned up against his car as Bill inspected the boat.

The boat was a mess. It was obvious it had been out of the water for quite a long time. While filthy, even Bill could see that the topsides and cabin only just needed some soap, some water, and some scrubbing. The interior was a different story. It was a train wreck. A wet, shitty, smelly, awful mess. The engine was dead, but that was of little relevance. It would have to go, anyway. Plus, with all the modifications and conversions that would need to be made, the interior would have to be gutted, too.

The broker had his arms crossed, waiting for the British guy to get done with his inspection. He wasn't expecting much to come from this viewing. He looked at his watch, closed his eyes, and mumbled, "Come on, fella. Hurry the hell up and stop wasting my time."

He's shown the boat many times before with all previous prospects saying, "I'll have to call you back." Or... "I'll have to think about it." Or even worse... "Let me talk to my wife." All of which are code words for, *Nope. I'm done here.*

The broker's disposition changed when he saw the smiling Brit emerge on deck and ask, "Does she float?"

The broker stood up taller, and with ninety-five percent certainty, said, "Of course."

"Then she's perfect!" said Bill. "But I can't pay what you're asking."

"That is fine," said the broker. "Only a fool pays full price. I can't get the moon unless I ask for it. Come on down and let's talk."

Twenty-three minutes later, Bill Salisbury was the new owner of a crappy old boat. But he would change all that.

10

C harlene recovered well. She remained in Tennessee for another five years, working and loving that grandbaby. Those were the two things that helped to distract her mind from losing me. No matter how I tried to encourage her to move on, she remained too damn stubborn. I had to find a way.

Her friends worried about her too. They wanted to see Charlene happy and get on with her life. And for a while, she saw other men, mostly guys introduced to her by friends. None of them lasted very long.

One time she went to the house of a friend, Betty. They worked together at the boutique. Betty and her husband, Ted, invited Charlene to dinner. While they were eating, Betty said, "Charlene, there is someone I'd like for you to meet. He's an accountant and…"

Charlene dropped her fork. "Just stop, Betty. Forget about it. I've tried seeing other people. They all seem like freaks and weirdos. I'm not up to that nonsense anymore."

"But Charlene… this one's…"

"This one's nothing. I'm done."

Betty said nothing.

"Look… I know you are just trying to help. But don't, because it doesn't. One day, maybe. Not today."

Betty gave a little huff. "Well, let me say one more thing."
Charlene said nothing.

"It's been over ten years, girl. Don't lose track of time."

Charlene said nothing, but Ted said, "Would somebody pass me the creamed potatoes and peas, please?"

They ate in silence for the rest of the dinner and ended up in the living room sharing a bottle of wine. The casual chit-chat put Charlene at ease until Betty said, "Ted. We need to find Charlene a real rich man."

"No, you don't," said Charlene. "I don't need a rich man. Don't want a rich man. I just want a good man. That's all I need and want. I've had rich men in my life before, and that never made them any good."

"Damn," said Ted. "I've never heard a woman say something like that."

"Well." Charlene said, "It's true."

Ted looked at Betty and asked, "Did you marry me for my money?"

Betty rolled her eyes in the back of her head, and said, "If I had married into money, you'd be alone, warming up TV dinners every night."

Later that evening, while she was in bed with Zoey, Charlene thought about the conversations at Betty and Ted's. After shedding a few tears, she grabbed a couple of tissues and dried her eyes. Then, much like when she prayed for God to take away the cigarettes, she closed her eyes and said, "Dear God. I am living proof that you answer prayers. And I don't want to sound selfish, but I could use your help again. I'm lonely. I don't want to be alone anymore. Please, Lord, bring a good man into my life. All I'm praying for is a man with a good heart. If there is one out there, I pray you send him my way. Amen."

I watched Charlene slide away into slumber. She looked

peaceful and calm, so I whispered in her ear. "We're trying, Charlie, but you have to let me go."

Her eyes opened and darted around the room. Then she shook her head and whispered, "I'm going crazy."

***

Three weeks later, I finally made a little progress with Charlene. She dropped in unannounced at her sister's house to visit, have coffee, and maybe go out to lunch. They were having a good time together, sitting around chatting it up. They were having a delightful time. I hoped to make it better.

That's when Jolene's cell phone rang on the kitchen counter. She got up to answer it. She looked at the screen and said, "That's odd."

"What?"

"It's Delta."

"Your psychic?"

"Yes. She never calls me."

Jolene answered the phone and turned away to talk. "My, my. If it isn't my Dahling Delta." She chuckled and continued. "Since you're calling me, do I get to charge you by the minute?"

"Consider this a freebee, Jolene," said Delta, "if you can help me get rid of this guy. He has annoyed the shit out of me all day."

"Who?"

"Says his name is Matt, Mark, or Mike. Something like that. Does it make sense to you?"

"No, not really."

"It has to mean something. He keeps saying, 'She's there.

She's there.'"

Jolene slowly turned around to look at Charlene, who had no interest in the conversation.

Delta said, "Yes! He said she is the one. He is excited. It's her."

"Yeeeeah," said Jolene. "My sister is here."

Charlene looked up. "What?"

"Great," said Delta. "He's nodding his head."

"Her late husband's name was Michael."

Charlene scrunched her eyebrows. "What's going on, Jolene?"

Jolene stayed on the line listening to her personal psychic, then she looked at her sister, covered the mouthpiece, and said, "It's Michael. He's with Delta."

"Hogwash. You know I don't believe in that nonsense."

Jolene listened some more, then said, "He has a message for you."

Charlene rolled her eyes and said nothing.

"Delta says he's smiling, holding up his hands, and wiggling his fingers."

"Knock it off, dammit. What are you trying to do?"

"Nothing. She called me, remember?"

It hit Charlene like a load of bricks. She had been with Jolene since she arrived. The entire time. Jolene had no idea she was dropping by the house. Charlene looked down at the kitchen table, gasped, and said, "I can't believe this."

Delta says he's quite animated about it.

Charlene covered her mouth. "He's telling me his hands don't hurt anymore."

Jolene sat next to her sister, put the phone on speaker, and repeated what Charlene had said.

"That's right," said Delta. "He's nodding his head. Okay...

wait. There's more. Now he's saying something about candy. Candy."

"Oh my God. He knows about the candy store I opened."

Delta said, "Yes. He's nodding. Now he is asking about the baby. Did you two have a child?"

Charlene was about to say no, but Delta interrupted, "Sorry. No. No. No. He's shaking his head. So, what baby could he be talking about?"

Tears welled up in her eyes, and as they streamed down her cheek, she said, "My granddaughter. She was born right before he died."

"That's the one. He's nodding his head."

Charlene was speechless, wiping the happy tears from her face.

"He seems thrilled now," said Delta. "Wait. One last thing. He's saying something about time. It's time, maybe. Yes. That's it. He's nodding his head. What does that mean?"

Charlene said nothing, but thought, *He's telling me to let go.*

"Okay, that's it," said Delta. "He seems happy, clapping, and walking away. He's gone."

Charlene still said nothing.

Three weeks later, the urge to return to Georgia became too great. She didn't want to leave Misty and Ophelia, but she felt the need. She gave her two-week notice at work and packed her bags. She was southbound.

11

CHICAGO: SUMMER 2017

After Bill bought the Carver in 2013, he spent several afternoons a week, plus weekends, working on it. With so much to do, it was a long process. Essentially, he had to plan out and rebuild the entire boat. But none of that could happen until he had a clear idea of what he had to work with. And that vision wouldn't be possible until the mess and awful smell were gutted and removed from the boat. The demolition began. If he couldn't salvage something, or it wasn't structural, to the dumpster it went. The hardest and dirtiest part was the removal of the engine.

It took several weeks to complete, but once he found himself with a clean shell of a boat, he focused on putting it back together to his liking. This was the fun part for Bill. Any monkey can tear something apart, but rebuilding it into a better version of itself takes planning, vision, and skill.

The rebuild took most of two years, and in 2015 he named the boat *Think or Swim*, splashed it in Lake Michigan and brought it down to Chicago. It was the most unique cruiser on the entire lake. She was totally electric and self-sufficient. No fossil fuels anywhere aboard. If need be, she could sever ties with civilization and her massive solar panels would feed the heart of the system, her high-capacity lithium battery bank.

The two years of floating and cruising on Lake Michigan gave Bill the time and experience needed to get to know his boat inside and out. Having installed all the systems himself, he was comfortable with the boat's capabilities, but putting them all into motion as a complete unit was a little different. He wanted to know every aspect of how she would behave in various conditions. During the summer of 2017, he felt he and his new girl were ready to set out on the grand adventure to navigate the waterways from the lake to the warm, blue waters of the Gulf of Mexico and destinations unknown.

He carefully studied the charts and practical destinations for layovers. He studied the locations and procedures to enter and exit the several dams and locks that lay between Chicago and the great Mississippi. It was time to throw caution to the wind.

On August 17th, 2017, Bill locked up his house, provisioned *Think or Swim*, and shoved off to start his slow journey south. Adrenaline fed his odd but pleasurable mixture of excitement and anxiety, an emotion he hadn't felt in a long time. He was happy.

The three hundred twenty-seven-mile journey out of Chicago to the Mississippi is broken up into sections, beginning with a short leg that navigates through the city and into the Chicago Sanitary and Ship Canal. Just before joining the Des Plaines River some thirty miles downstream, Bill got his first taste of locking through at the Lockport Dam. The experience of dropping the required fifteen feet to the new river level was both exciting and without drama. In short order, he was locking through again at Brandon Road. By the time he locked through Dresden Island Dam and joined the Illinois River, he had become an old hat at navigating the locks.

The Illinois River is the longest stretch down to the town of Grafton, where it feeds into the Mississippi. Approximately two hundred seventy-three miles. He took his time and enjoyed the trip going downstream. Some of the scenery was breathtaking. He was in no huge hurry. But in truth, he had little choice. *Think or Swim's* limited propulsion curbed her capacity to about five knots of speed over the ground, but he didn't press or overwork the engines. So, with the help of the river, he averaged about five and a half to six knots. The best part, he quickly learned after several days underway, was that he had no place to be except for wherever he was at. It was a better freedom than he ever expected to feel. If work came to call, or if the weather simply wasn't cooperating for a safe passage, he would either drop a hook in a safe anchorage or tie up as a transient at one of the several marinas along the way.

The sun was dropping fast one afternoon, and there was no way he would make Peoria before dark, so he searched the chart for a safe place to settle for the evening. He decided on ducking into a protected nook called Sawmill Lake near the Township of Henry, Illinois. After cleaning up from dinner, he relaxed in the salon and realized that he had never been happier. He later moved to the aft deck to enjoy the evening and think.

When he left Chicago, he openly joked that he was leaving it all behind and would never come back. The rational and intelligent part of him knew that probably wouldn't be the case. But as he swung on the hook, listening to music and sipping wine, those parts of his intellect surreptitiously agreed with his heart. It was then he knew. He would return to Chicago occasionally, but only for work. He would break off all other permanent ties. It was a thought that warmed his heart.

After a couple of hours, he went inside and put water on the stove to make tea. Later, as he bounced the tea bags in the hot liquid, his phone rang. A quick glance at his watch told him it was a few minutes after ten. "Ah," he said. "Running a little late." It was the New Delhi office, calling in for their morning conference call. It was time to go to work. He answered the phone. "Running a little late, are we?"

Whatever the response, it made him chuckle. "Oh, no. I'm in grand spirits. Top of the morning to you. So, let's get started. Where are we?"

***

The next morning, Bill pulled up his anchor and started back down the river. The work call from the night before only lasted about an hour and a half. With six solid hours of sleep under his belt, he felt rested. It was lazy and pleasurable progress, but as he and *Think or Swim* slipped through the water, resolute that he was done with Chicago, there was one thing he couldn't leave behind. His plane. He figured he could always wait until he finally landed someplace, but when and where would that be? He didn't know. His plans, or intentions, were to follow the route of the Great Loop. If or when the right place came along, he would stick around. In his mind, he thought about South Florida. That would be a lengthy trip. *What if I need it sooner than that?* He wasn't comfortable being separated from his aircraft, so he studied the charts and formulated a plan.

A few days later, he neared the point where the Illinois River flowed into the grand Mississippi, but it would have to wait. It was late morning. Bill called ahead to the river marina in Grafton, Illinois, and reserved a transient slip for a few days. After tying up in his temporary slip, he went to the Grafton Oyster Bar for lunch. After ordering his meal, he made another call to Smartt Field, the St. Charles County Regional Airport. The airstrip was in Missouri, just a ferry ride across the river and an Uber away. The next morning, he rented a car and drove back to Chicago.

***

Of the two possible routes south, Bill picked the lazier and more picturesque, leaving the Mississippi to run up the Ohio to catch the Cumberland River and down through Kentucky Lake, into the Tennessee River, then the beautiful, winding Tombigbee, and ultimately the Mobile River that would deliver him and his vessel in the mouth of Mobile Bay.

All along the way, his routine was simple: take a few days to cruise down the rivers, find a suitable spot to stop, grab a rental, and go fetch his plane. Back and forth. Back and forth. It was tiring, but fun at the same time and became part of the adventure. Yes, it slowed his progress to the Gulf of Mexico, but again, he wasn't in any hurry. And in the end, it was worth it.

12

The Devil Wears Prada

C harlene went back home to Donalsonville. While she still distanced herself from the idea of other men, she didn't pine over my passing as much as before. She kept busy, and it was fun watching her come into her own. With her southern sassy demeanor, and to the great chagrin of many locals, she set out to take her little, boring hometown and turn it upside down. It all started when she and her sister Sarah opened a wine and specialty shop in the middle of town. It wasn't a liquor bar, just a wine-tasting shop. However, you couldn't tell by the reception it got from those deeply rooted in the Bible Belt of South Georgia. The local school board wasn't happy with her either. She just wanted to bring some fun to her little town, but some viewed her as a troublemaker. The demon on Second Street. A sister of sin.

Then she turned up the heat. While serving on the board at the Chamber of Commerce, she got involved with the Downtown Development Authority. And during one meeting, as the group completed some details that would bring in local artists to paint murals on some of the building walls, she interrupted the proceeding and changed the subject.

"That's all sweet and good. I'm sure those murals will be quite pretty and all, but don't y'all get tired of this little town being so slow and stodgy?"

They looked at her with blank stares.

"I mean come on," she said. "When was the last time this town had some real fun? And don't bring up the Easter Hop and Shop, the Fall Pumpkin Patch, or that goofy Five and Twelve K Fun Run. Dear God... since when was exercise ever fun? I tried it once. Ice cubes kept sloshing out of my cocktail."

They met her comments with silence again until the chairman asked, "Well, Charlene. What do you have in mind?"

She leaned in close, as if to share a little secret, and said, "A party. A party for the people of this town. A proper party, with live music and everything."

Someone else asked, "Where would we do this... party?"

Charlene grinned and said, "In town. We'll close off some streets and have us a big shindig."

All the other board members looked at each other.

"What are you scared of... a little fun? Come on, don't be such tight-ass ninnies."

And that is how Donalsonville got their first-ever downtown New Year Eve's party, complete with a little disco ball to drop at the magic hour. The roads around Charlene's shop were closed off, a band came in to set up at one end, and the bistro across the street served killer food. Other restaurants set up tents to offer their brand of fare. They even got special permission to allow folks to meander around with their favorite adult beverages. And something marvelous happened. The people came. Everybody. It was a raving success.

Before the night was over, Charlene and other board members were fielding questions about when the next party would be. Those questions gave birth to their first Mardi Gras celebration, then later a St. Patrick's Day event. She had unleashed a sleeping giant of festive celebration, and when the local church folks weren't dancing and having a good time, Charlene might as well have been Miranda Priestly from *The Devil Wears Prada*.

Either way, Charlene grew tired of being the local punching bag. All she ever wanted was for her little town to let down its hair and cut loose a little, not sacrifice puppies and kittens in the town square. And while she delivered on her dreams, she also got fed up with having to defend herself all the time. It was time for a change. Little did she know that change would mean Port St. Joe.

Both her sister, Jolene, and daughter, Madelyn, had purchased some investment property on Fourth Street in the sleepy coastal town. A cluster of small short-term rentals perfect for vacationing tourists. Still in Tennessee, they needed somebody to stay on the property and manage the units. Charlene was up to it and ready for a change, so she packed her bags and headed to the beach.

13

MOBILE BAY AND BEYOND

B ill's adventures down the network of waterways were exciting and picturesque. The sights were lovely, and the southerly stray down the Tombigbee and Mobile Rivers was beautiful. The further south he traveled, the more complex the waterways became. He was entering the expansive and meandering Mobile Delta. Second only to the Mississippi Delta, it covers over 20,300 acres of water. Stretching 30 miles long and 12 miles wide, it comprises over 200,000 acres of swamps and marshes. Considered one of the country's natural wonders, it earned the Congressional designation as a National Nature Landmark, a highly coveted honor. To Bill, the waterway did not disappoint.

However, the further he traveled down the river, the more obvious it became that he and his boat were transitioning from natural wonder to industrialized civilization. While not uncommon to see and pass tugs and barges along his route, now he was seeing more barges, rows of barges moored in the channel, waiting to be loaded or offloaded. Before long, the hustle and bustle of the commercial marine traffic and the City of Mobile surrounded him. It was a stark reminder that, while the simple and beautiful backcountry existed, the full-blown activity of commerce and industry still drove the life and economy of society. While not very attractive, it was necessary. And while necessary, it was only temporary.

After passing the busy loading and unloading at the Alabama Port Authority, Little Sand Island, and finally the steady overhead air traffic launching from the Mobile Airport, he found himself in the middle of the beautiful Mobile Bay. And the further he cruised into the bay, the easier it became to let his mind wander from the realities of life to visions of more pleasant surroundings.

After shifting to a southeasterly heading, he made his way toward the cozy town of Fairhope and the Dock Marina, where he had already called ahead and made slip arrangements. Once settled and after grabbing a bite to eat, he wasted no time getting a rental car to go check out the small, one runway airstrip that would be the Fairhope Airport. He found it all satisfactory and made storage reservations to keep his bird there while he pressed on with the boat.

The drive up to Columbus, Mississippi, where he last left the plane, was a tiring one. But the flight down was worth every painful hour he spent enduring the shittiest roads he had ever driven on. Once he was off the ground, he was rewarded, especially as his flight plan took him directly over the Mobile Delta. On the chart, the network of rivers, creeks, swamps, and marshes was impressive, but from the air, the view was... well, heavenly. It seemed to stretch as far as the eye could see, and its beauty was evidence of what millions of years of natural waterway sculpting could achieve. It took his breath away.

After three days of work and relaxation in Fairhope, Bill got the itch to press on. Before turning in on the last night, he sat down with his charts to forge his plan. Based on the waypoints he selected for his route down the bay, the eastern mouth of the Intracoastal at Oyster Bay was roughly twenty-five nautical miles. He had already informed the Harbormaster he would pull out the next morning and paid his fees in full. With all that settled, if he got underway by six in the morning, and could average four and a half to five knots over the ground, he would enter Portage Creek at Oyster Bay before noon. From there, he could venture eastward to the next destination that he found on the chart. Pirate's Cove, some fifteen nautical miles away on the shores of Josephine, Alabama.

He gave a wave goodbye to nobody as he left the channel at Fairhope. Once *Think or Swim* arrived at her southwestern waypoint, the autopilot made the adjustments to bring her around to a southeasterly course of 140 degree true, but a stiff headwind coming in from the Gulf of Mexico along with a steady chop slowed her progress down to at or below four knots. There is only so much that her electrical propulsion can do.

A little after one in the afternoon, he arrived at the mouth of Portage Creek and the ICW. Now, being in the shoreline's lee, the effects of the breeze diminished, and the boat behaved much better. Even so, he slowed the girl down to enjoy the ride. Plus, he was getting hungry, so he picked up a slip and grabbed a sandwich at Lulu's. He didn't realize until he was seated and having his lunch that Lulu was the sister of Jimmy Buffett, not that he was much of a Parrot Head to begin with. While having lunch, he met a few other boaters and inquired about the place he found on the charts, Pirate's Cove. Everyone he spoke with assured him he would love it. And virtually everyone commented, even insisted, that having one of their burgers was a must.

Bill checked the charts and figured the distance to Pirate's Cove to be about ten miles. Even if he took his sweet time, he could be there well before his scheduled conference call with the Chicago office. So off he went, silently down the channel. And while Portage Creek is plenty wide for navigational purposes, it was a very busy waterway, so you had to be diligent in operation. But if there was one thing this part of the passage gave him, it was a heightened appreciation for the quiet operation of his electric propulsion. Being buzzed by jet skis and other loud and obnoxious crafts like cigarette boats and Donzi craft wore on his nerves. He couldn't wait to exit the creek and enter the broader sections of Wolf Bay and Bay La Launch.

Pirate's Cove was busy, but he found space to tie up *Think or Swim* out on the end of the courtesy dock. The place was buzzing with people. And as suggested, he ordered the burger. It was excellent. As he walked back out to his boat to prepare for his call, he noticed several folks gathered around looking at his boat, pointing and commenting on all the solar panels. This was something he had become accustomed to. He understood his boat was quite a novelty, so he has a well-prepared and rehearsed brief on the boat's system, battery capacity, propulsion, and performance. People are quite dumbfounded to learn he navigated all the way from Lake Michigan without burning one dinosaur.

The conference call went well. All projects and customers are happy. The sales team picked up a few new clients, and everybody was thrilled with the growth. As the call ended, the head of marketing in the US office requested that Bill give him a buzz so they could chat offline. Bill rolled his eyes because he was sure of the subject. The last time they chatted, Jerry bombarded him with questions and inquiries about his love life and female companionship.

"Okay, Jerry," said Bill. "But I don't have a lot of time," he lied. "I will get underway soon."

Jerry answered on the first ring. "Hey, buddy. How's it hanging?"

Another eye roll. "The last time I checked, it was hanging just fine."

"You're down by the coast now. The eye candy down there must be fantastic."

And it was, tanned bodies and bikinis everywhere. Especially on the boats that would pass by, from the flying bridge there was no shortage of shapely gals to gaze at.

"I'd be lying, Jerry, if I said, 'Not really.'"

"I knew it! Ha. Man, I'm jealous. Have you met anybody?"

"I've met many people."

"Damn, Bill. You know what I'm talking about."

"Jerry, why are you so damn concerned about my sex life?"

"I'm not worried about it, man. I just know how you are. A damn workaholic, and I know that trip down the river must get lonely."

Bill got to thinking. Jerry was right. He loved to work. It was just how his mind was wired. But, if he had to admit it, there were several times when he would have loved to have had some female companionship. Just to share the experience, if nothing else.

"Bill? Bill? Are you still there?"

"Yes, Jerry. I'm here, so what else is it I can do for you? I need to get moving."

"It isn't what you can do for me. It's what I have done for you. I know you are busy working and playing Tom Sawyer on the water. And I know you don't have a lot of time to socialize and meet gals. So... I've made it easier for you. Hold on, let me send you an email with a link."

A few seconds later, Bill's computer dinged. He opened the email and clicked on the link. "What the hell is this, Jerry?"

"Don't thank me now, but it's a link to your Tinder account. It's an app for meeting people. I set a profile up for you. Now you can find chicks, hot chicks in your area that would love to meet you and hook up. Dude, the account has only been open a few days, and you should see all the traffic you're getting. But that's just up here in Chicago. Once you login to your account, your location will update via your IP address. Then the local gals will see you, you'll probably start getting swipes pretty soon."

"Swipes?"

"Yeah, Bill. If you like somebody's profile, you swipe right on their picture. If you'd rather pass, you swipe left. I suggest you download the app on your phone as well, so you can have it with you all the time. Plus, via the app, the location is more precise since it uses the GPS to track your location."

"You seem quite the expert, Jerry."

"Well, yeah. I have an account. I'm swiping my ass off every day."

Jerry gave Bill his username and password, and he wrote it down. Not sure why.

"Listen, Jerry. I don't know. I appreciate your help. I really do..."

"Don't give me that, blah blah blah crap. Promise me you'll try it. Trust me, you'll thank me for it later."

"Okay, Jerry. I promise. But I got to go."

"Let me know how it goes, okay?"

"Sure Jerry, bye."

Bill ended the call and slouched back in his chair. His eyes wandered to his computer screen, and he saw some of the attractive women that had shown interest. He scrolled through them until he shook his head and closed the laptop with a smack. "Bloody hell!"

14

CHARLENE IN ST. JOE

C harlene was proud of her sister and daughter. They had done well in their little vacation rental village. Three cottages together on Fourth Street. She stayed in one unit while booking and keeping up with the others. It was fun, and it didn't take long for the phone to ring. Before she knew it, the units were booked well in advance on the calendar.

When she arrived in St. Joe, she knew not a soul, except for the tourists that made Fourth Street their home for a week or two. But that was okay, for two reasons. For one, she was busy, so there wasn't much time to socialize. For another, she has never known a stranger. People were already friends with Charlene. They just didn't know it yet. She has that type of infectious personality. Then, if she were to learn that you were from South Georgia, Charlene would go into her conversational genealogy. "Who's your momma? Who's your grandma?" Either of those questions would almost always give birth to a connection somewhere in the theoretical six degrees of separation. It didn't take long before Charlene's network of friends grew. She wasn't alone anymore.

Things in the vacation village were running smoothly. So much so that she sought additional employment to help pass the time and to make more money. She was thankful for the income from managing the properties, but the pay wasn't quite enough to satisfy her passion for fashion. And my oh my, how that Charlene loves some clothes. That was one thing from our short marriage I didn't miss. Ha!

Anyway, after casually examining her options in town, which were few, luck shined down on her. It was a match made in heaven. A high-end women's boutique on Reid Avenue was hiring, and Charlene had the perfect retail experience. It was a win-win for all involved.

And that was how Charlene's life took shape in Port St. Joe. She enjoyed meeting and taking care of the clients at the rentals, and she loved working at the boutique. She especially loved her new network of girlfriends. On days after work, she and her gang could often be found at the marina Dockside Grill, sipping wine and taking in sunsets. That is what the locals do down there. Stop the hustle and bustle and watch the fireball drop. Rarely does it disappoint.

Sure, Charlene went out with a few men. But it was always the same. Exhausting and dull, with lackluster results. She finally gave up and fell into that lifestyle, often adopted by widows, where comfort and strength of companionship is found with the girls. It wasn't a great life, but it wasn't a bad one either.

15

LOVE ME TINDER

B ill eased along across the eastern end of Choctawhatchee Bay on autopilot and cleared Pilcher Park at the Highway 331 bridge. Three miles ahead lay the mouth of the next section of the Intracoastal that would lead him and his boat to West Bay and the area surrounding Panama City. With less than a mile to go, his cell phone rang. He looked at the screen. It was his real estate agent in Chicago.

"Mindy! How are you?"

"Hello, Bill. Do you have a minute?"

Bill looked around at the gorgeous day and the beautiful water. The electric motors were as quiet as ever. The only sound was the gentle separation of water from the bow wave forward. He checked the speed of his boat. An easy four knots, and he chuckled. "I don't know Mindy. Things are pretty hectic around here at the moment, but I think I can squeeze in a little time for you. What's up?"

"I have a contract on your house."

Bill pulled back on the throttle and the boat slowed and coasted. "A contract? You're kidding me? I thought you said the market was saturated with inventory and it could take months."

"It is, and yes, that's what I said, but that didn't seem to matter."

"What are the terms? What do they want?"

"Not *they*, *him*. Pending an inspection, full asking, and you pay closing?"

"How does the buyer look? Does it appear he qualifies?"

"Don't know. I haven't seen his wallet."

"His wallet?"

"It's a cash deal, Bill. And he wants to close as soon as possible."

"Did you say, cash?"

"Cash. You live a charmed life, Bill. I'm sending you the contract now. Give it your eSignature and we'll get the ball rolling."

"Bloody hell. Cash, you say?"

"Yes, Bill. You heard it right the second time, too. So... answer one little question for me."

"Shoot."

"How soon can you have your ass up here to move your shit out of this guy's house?"

***

Three days later, Jerry came into the office and immediately noticed the light on in Bill's office, and the door cracked. He tilted his head, walked over, rapped on the door with his knuckles, and went in. "Is there something I can help you... Bill? What the hell are you doing here? I thought you were still down on the coast."

"I was. Left the boat in Panama City for a few weeks." Bill looked at his watch. "You're late. Is this what happens when I'm not around?"

"No! Not at all. Late night, that's all. Did you say, 'a few weeks?'"

"Got a buyer for the house and we close in three weeks. I need to move out and have my stuff put in storage. Plus, it will be good for me to be back in the office for a while."

"Oh," said Jerry. "So how long is, a while?"

Bill looked up from the reports he was reading. "As long as it takes, Jerry."

"Sure. Sure. Of course." Jerry grabbed a chair, sat down, and looked around to see if anybody was listening in. "So, tell me. How is that Tinder account working for you?"

Bill looked up. "The what?"

"You got to be kidding me, Bill. The Tinder account." Jerry shook his head. "Are you telling me you haven't used it to hook up with a little strange?"

Bill's look of confusion was replaced with one of agitated familiarity. He went back to looking at reports. "Oh, that thing. No, I haven't given it another thought."

"Son of a bitch, Bill. I'm just trying to help you out. And besides, you promised you would try it."

Bill looked back up and changed the subject. "I have work to do." He placed a finger on his chin to think. "Oh, and that probably means you have work to do, too. I think that's how it works."

Jerry stood up. "Suit yourself. I was just trying to help a brother out."

"And I appreciate it. Really..." Bill spun his chair to turn his back on Jerry and face the window to look out over Lake Michigan. "...but based on these latest reports, you could be a bigger help by getting your team to bring in some damn new business. Please close the door on your way out." Moments later, Bill's eyes winced as he heard the latch strike home a little louder than normal. Bill continued to gaze at numbers on the report, but he wasn't studying them at all. He finally dropped it in his lap and watched the boats move about the water. "Damn. I miss my boat."

***

Six weeks later, everything had been settled. The house closed, stuff was in storage, and details with the company had been sorted out. Even Jerry brought in three new accounts from large multi-corporate firms. Bill was happy, and the itch to get back on the water ate at him. He opened his laptop and pulled up MarineWays.com to study and plan the next leg of his voyage. He couldn't wait to get underway. With the route planner, he drew the course. Starting at St. Andrews Marina, where *Think or Swim* patiently waited, he studied the channel across the bay into East Bay and into the backlands of the ICW. He made note of some of the landmarks along the way: Overstreet, White City, Lake Wimico, and Apalachicola Bay. Once outside Apalachicola Bay, he would have to navigate the channel through St. George Sound all the way into the Carrabelle River and up to the town named for the same.

This last stretch is vast and quite exposed to the elements of the Gulf of Mexico and protected only by the barrier islands of St. George and Dog Island. He knew making the trip in one attempt would not happen, but he wanted to get the lay of the land for his own sake.

Getting to Carrabelle was important. Once there, he would need to pick his weather window carefully before setting out again. Once you clear Carrabelle, the protections of the ICW end. The next leg is an open water passage across the Gulf to

Tarpon Springs. A 140 nautical mile passage that can get quite lumpy in any weather.

Bill and his plane touched down at the Apalachicola Regional Airport three days later. He considered flying into Panama City, but figured it made more sense to advance the plane closer to Carrabelle. He gave the airstrip in Carrabelle a gander but decided on the more substantial resources of the Apalach Regional.

As he completed the arrangements to keep the plane on the premises, his Happy Trail taxi waited. When he climbed into the back of the cab, the driver, a middle-aged female with dark hair and gray root highlights, turned and asked, "Where to?"

Bill looked at his watch. It was 11:10 in the morning. That made it 10:10 in Panama City. "I'll tell you what. What is your name?"

"Carol."

"Very nice. Carol, do you know how to get to Uncle Ernie's?"

"The restaurant in Panama?"

"Exactly. Yes. Take me there and I'll buy you lunch. It's a good day to be back in Florida."

"You want to buy me lunch?"

"Well, I want to get back to my boat. It's there at the marina. Lunch is just a gesture to say thanks."

"Hey, pal. I have a boyfriend, you know."

"No, I didn't know that. But call him. He can come along as well."

"That's a mighty pretty accent you got there, mister... mister..."

"I'm sorry. The name is Bill. I'm British."

"You kinky or something?"

"You are too funny, Carol. I'm just in a good mood. If we get going, we make the restaurant before the big lunch crowd."

It was a delightful lunch and from where they sat, he could see his boat. It was a joyful sight. Bill got to learn more about Carol than he would have cared to, but being British and polite to a fault, he feigned his interest in her life story. Born and raised in Eastpoint, she got pregnant by Ned, her current boyfriend, at the age of sixteen. Two more kids later, the love never ceased. They have been together ever since. It's been a fairytale existence. Ned came from a long line of oystermen, tonging the beds of Apalachicola Bay for generations. It was the only industry they knew. An industry that had fallen on some bad luck in recent times. A combination of drought, flooding, and over-harvesting in the wake of the Deep Horizon oil disaster left the beds decimated. And there is even talk that the state may close the bay to all harvesting if conditions don't improve.

Bill stood as Carol rose to leave. She thanked him for the lunch and the generous tip, and he remained standing until she exited the building. As he sat back down, his waitress, Tina, came by to check on him.

"Can I get you anything else, or are you set?"

"Please bring me another one of these." He raised his pint glass. "And what did you say it was called?"

"That's my favorite. It's a Dirty Blonde."

"Sounds scandalous, but it's very tasty."

Tina chuckled, reached behind her neck, and flipped her blond ponytail over her front left shoulder. "Yeah. Like me. Hold on. I'll get you another."

Bill watched her walk away. It was a good walk. A very good walk. And for a moment, a desire for female companionship seeped into his brain.

He was reluctant, but he opened the Tinder app on his

phone and scrolled through the meat market. *How did this work again? Swipe left if you like them.* He gave a random picture a swipe to the left, and it was rejected. "Oops!" he said to the screen. "Sorry about that."

He continued to scroll through the pictures. The mix of fine-looking ladies compared to those with looks of desperation ran about fifty-fifty. Tina brought his beer, and he shut down the app, feeling stupid.

"Are you okay?" she asked.

"I'm fine. I was just thinking of something utterly stupid. Thank you for the beer. Bring me my check whenever you get around to it."

She pulled the ticket from her apron, placed it on the table, smiled, offered a *Have a nice day*, and left.

Again, he watched her leave, and the walk was good.

His gaze was interrupted by an intentional, attention-getting cough. He looked up and found a beautiful woman standing at his table. She had shoulder-length red hair and piercing green eyes. She wore a short beige, open-back halter dress that left little to the imagination of her deep cleavage, slim waist, and long legs. To top everything else, her skin was perfectly tanned, from her hairline to her barefoot, pedicured toes.

She gave a little pout. "Bill. You sure know how to hurt a girl."

Breathe, dammit. Breathe. He gave a little gasp. "Excuse me?"

"Did you not like what you saw?"

"Excuse me," he said. "I'm so sorry. I don't understand what you are talking about."

She held up her phone. "This is you, isn't it?"

Bill leaned in closer for a better look and immediately

realized he was looking at his profile picture on her Tinder app. He sat back in his chair with a slump. *Oh, dear.* He held his breath again.

"Well?" she said.

Breathe! He gave a puff. "Yes. That is me. But..."

"I saw you online just a few minutes ago. I was sitting right over there." She pointed to a table across the room. "I'm guessing you came across my profile since we were in such proximity."

"Umm.... umm. I... I'm not sure. I don't use the thing much and... and... You see..."

"I *see* you already have a beer. May I join you?"

Bill stood up, knocking his chair back and almost flipping the table. His beer slid toward the edge, but she grabbed it before it spilled.

It was an awkward moment. "Yes, please. Be my guest." They both sat down. She took a small sip of his beer, then handed it to him.

"Nice catch. By the way. Thanks."

She smiled.

"Oh, dear. Excuse me. You must be thirsty. May I offer you something?"

"I'll have a Dirty Blonde, too."

In a flash of comedic genius, Bill ran his palm over his shiny bald head and said, "I'm sorry. I can't help you in that department."

They both shared a great laugh. A fun and genuine laugh. When it ended, Bill smiled, waved Tina over to the table, and looked over his shoulder at his boat. *Sorry, girl. You're going to have to wait a little bit longer.*

And that is how Bill met Carla.

Bill and Carla chatted for hours. Tina, the waitress, didn't mind because they kept ordering drinks. What started out as a friendly lunch with a nice, but worn-out taxi driver resulted in an early dinner with a red-headed bombshell. My, how his luck had changed. And yes, it was good to be back in Florida. She shared a lot about herself. Born in Destin and moved to Panama City with her mother when she was six after her father removed himself from their lives. She grew up in old Panama City and hates Panama City Beach, except for the rolls of money she makes off that section of town. She sells real estate there. A lot of real estate, mainly resort condos as investment vacation properties. She also owned several oceanfront rental units up and down Thomas Drive. She's quite successful. She was so successful that Bill wondered why she needed an app like Tinder to meet people. So, diplomatically, he asked.

"I don't know," she said. "I like to meet people and it's kind of a fun idea. And nothing is permanent with Tinder. I'm not looking for permanent."

Bill gave her a little background and told her of his plans and adventures. "I'm basically making it up as I go along. How does it go? Round and round and round I go... Where I stop, nobody knows."

"Wow. That all sounds so exciting. It would be so cool to be free like that. Sometimes I feel like I'm stuck here."

Bill leaned forward. "You seem like you are successful enough. I'm guessing, but it seems like you make enough to take some time off. You should try it."

She leaned forward, too. "Is that an invite?"

Bill leaned back. "Huh?"

She leaned in even closer. "Is that an invitation, silly? To join you."

"On the boat?"

She leaned back. "I'm sorry. I thought..."

"No. I'm sorry. I was just saying that you should take some time off. I didn't mean to make it sound like..."

"So, you don't want me to come along?"

Bill raised a finger. "Now, dammit. I never said that either. Don't put words in my mouth."

"Okay, Bill. I like you. You seem to have a kind heart. And I don't mean to put you on the spot, but it seems a man of your means shouldn't need a Tinder account either."

"Now, about that. The thing is..."

"You don't have to explain anything. It's not important. The bottom line is, I think you sort of like me too. So, if you won't invite me to come along, I'll invite myself. What do you say?"

Bill was at a loss for words. He was looking for the right words. He rubbed his head in angst.

"And Bill..."

He looked straight into her eyes.

She lowered her head. "Nothing is permanent. Remember?"

Then, he found the one word he was looking for. "Okay."

16

CARLA

The next morning, Bill was preparing to get underway. As he tinkered around, he thought of the night he and Carla had shared. It was fun, and when she left around midnight, he expected to never see her again. Nothing is permanent. But as he was topping off the water tanks, he saw her smiling and walking down the dock. *Do all the gals walk that way in Florida?* She wore shorts and a furry sweater to hold off the morning chill. She carried a purse and a small overnight bag. As she approached, Bill said, "Right on time. I wondered if you would come."

She stopped, gave him a quick kiss on the cheek, and climbed aboard.

He watched her disappear into the cabin. "Make yourself at home."

At 10:00 am, with the help of a dockhand, the last line was cast, and the boat quietly eased away from the dock. Bill gazed at the chart plotter. He had a course of 23 nautical miles planned. That would just put them into the mouth of the ICW ditch and he had already identified a joining creek that would make a good place to stop for the night. It was late October. The days were already getting short, and he wanted to put some distance in the bank before nightfall. If he could average a speed of three and a half knots, they should have the hook down no later than four-thirty in the afternoon.

Carla emerged from the cabin. "Oh, my God. We're moving. Bill? Where are you?"

"Up here. On the flying bridge."

She joined him. She had lost the sweater and shorts and traded them for a bikini and a sheer, see-through swimsuit coverup. Bill noticed the morning air was still fresh enough for her nipples to respond.

"That was just too weird," she said. "I had no idea we had left the dock. The boat is so quiet."

"I told you last night. All electric propulsion. Peaceful, huh?"

"Maybe a little too peaceful. I'm used to boats with motors."

"She has a motor, it's just..." he could see his words weren't registering. "Never mind."

"I'm going to fix a drink. Can I get you anything?"

"No thanks. I'll come down later and make myself some tea."

"Suit yourself."

He watched her disappear and later re-emerge on the foredeck. She spread a beach towel on the forward cabin top, climbed up, lost the coverup and laid on her stomach. It was a distraction. Luckily, the autopilot would do most of the driving. When he had a nice open stretch ahead, he went below to heat some water. As he waited, he came out from time to time to check on things. Once he had his tea poured, he went back to the flying bridge. As he took his first sip, he gasped, sucked, and burned the back of his throat. "Damn," he uttered under his breath. Carla had turned over on her back and revealed the mysteries of her perfectly tanned breasts. The top was off.

"You're doing that on purpose!"

She smiled and nodded her head.

Bill spent the next couple of hours on a conference call. When it was done, he called down. "Are you getting hungry?"

She nodded her head.

"Make us some sandwiches and join me. Whatever you make is fine. You'll find everything in the galley."

She gave a thumbs-up, then got to her feet, leaving the bikini top and cover-up on deck. She joined him, still topless, carrying two plates, tuna fish sandwiches, and chips. "What can I get you to drink?" she asked.

"Just water for me."

She leaned in and kissed him. "You got it."

She returned with a glass of ice water for Bill and a fresh vodka drink for herself. She produced a joint and a lighter that had been tucked away in the front of her bikini bottom. She brought the joint to her lips and fired it up, taking in a healthy supply of smoke. Holding her breath, she offered it to Bill. He declined.

Still holding it, she said, "It's superb shit."

"No thanks. Not really into that."

She exhaled a cloud of smoke. "You don't know what you are missing. When I say good, I mean damn good."

"I'll have to trust you on that?"

She took another hit and held it. "You don't mind, though, do you?"

"Knock yourself out."

"Perfect."

And she did. And she did. And she did. Until it was time for a nap in the salon.

While she slept, Bill and the boat entered the mouth of the ditch. Off to port, he found what he was looking for, the mouth of Wetappo Creek. He eased in to get out of the channel. It was shallow, but he dropped the hook and found a good holding. They were safe.

When Carla finally woke up, the cabin lights were red. She got up and looked out. It was dark outside. The only white light was that of the anchor light to mark their position to other craft. She found Bill on the afterdeck, enjoying a Strongbow Cider.

"Where are we?" she asked.

"Oh... there you are. Good morning."

"Morning?"

"Just kidding. Early evening. About seven-thirty. I thought about waking you, but you looked so peaceful. Are you hungry?"

"Yes. Where are we?"

"Wetappo Creek. We are in for the night."

She looked around. "Where is the marina? I thought we would pull into a marina."

"It's a marina of one." He stood. "How do steaks on the grill sound?"

"We're gonna stay out here? All night? Where's the damn marina?"

"Carla, there is no marina. We don't need a marina. We have everything we need right here on the boat."

"I don't think I like this."

"I don't understand. This is like camping, better than camping, just on the water."

"I don't fucking like camping, dammit!"

"Easy now. Let me get some food started and you'll feel better. Just relax. It will be okay."

"The hell it will. Where's my weed?"

He watched her storm off and go inside. He never saw that

coming.

She returned while he cooked on the grill. She was back into her shorts and sweater; the air had cooled down considerably. She took hits on another joint as the meat cooked. That must have helped to take the edge off. She seemed to do better. The steaks and baked potatoes were good. She liked it, and they washed down the meal with a bottle of red wine.

It was a little after nine when they finished dinner and retreated to the salon. He wanted another Strongbow, and she wanted more vodka and cranberry and to fire up what was left of her joint. As she brought out the roach, he flung up a hand. "Not inside, please. I don't mind you smoking, but not inside."

She acted a little put out and huffed a little as she stepped out the cabin door. From inside, he watched the contrast of the red-hot end of the joint as she drew on it to the red interior cabin lighting. He counted four long draws. *Man, she is going to be wasted.*

When she returned, a sly grin stretched across her face. She looked great in the light. She approached and joined him on the settee, wrapping her arms around him and delivering a gentle kiss to his lips. "Why the red lights?" She kissed him on the neck.

"It is for night vision. Better to see, if..."

"Are you saying you can see me better like this? I have to admit, it is all a little sexy."

"Ahhh..." He realized there was no reason to explain. "If it makes you feel sexy, then I'm glad."

She leaned in for a long kiss, but before their lips touched, a blood-curdling scream erupted from outside the boat. Startled, they pulled away from each other.

"What in the hell was that?"

The screaming returned, along with a fighting growl. It sounded like it was on the boat. Carla jumped to her feet. "Dammit! What is going on?"

Bill stood as well. "I don't know. Sounds like wild animals."

And Bill hit the nail on the head. Two males, a bobcat and a coyote, found each other while prowling the shoreline on the creek. They were facing off, neither willing to back off, and they continued to warn the other.

"Wild animals! Oh, hell no! Get me the fuck out of here!"

"Calm down, it will be okay. They will stop soon."

But the predators didn't stop. They launched themselves into a full battle that seemed to last forever.

"YOU GOT TO BE SHITTING ME!" yelled Carla as the battle raged on.

Now Bill had to raise his voice. "Calm down, dammit! Go smoke some more of your damn weed or something."

"Screw you, Bill. I ain't going out there. What do you think I am, a damn fool?"

And just as fast as the National Geographic wildlife moment started, it stopped with an eerie silence. Just in time for Bill to yell, "A fool? No. Batshit crazy? Yes!"

They stood in the salon, looking at each other. Then she rushed by him, retreated to the aft cabin, slammed the door and locked it. As much of a sexy bombshell as she was, Bill stood, relieved to be out of her presence. He slowly walked to the door and asked, "Does this mean I'm not getting laid?"

It sounded like she was just on the other side of the door when she yelled back. "Get me off this fucking boat!"

Bill smiled and went to the galley for another Strongbow.

17

DANNY: GOVERNOR OF WHITE CITY

I t was a beautiful morning. The sun was just coming up as the anchor windlass steadily and with ceremonious clamor deposited the chain into the anchor locker. As the boat drifted free, Bill took the hose and rinsed the mud off the plow anchor. Once clean, it was time to get underway.

An hour or so later, Carla joined Bill on the flying bridge. This time with a new sweater. If she had anything beneath it, he couldn't tell. There were no apologies or words spoken about the night before.

"How long have we been moving?" she asked.

"About an hour and a half?" Bill was stoic in his tone, and after a good sip of tea, he said, "The coffee pot is ready to go, if you want some. Just turn it on."

"Thanks."

Bill turned to see her rub her eyes and head down to the galley. She joined him later with a big mug of hot, steaming coffee. She blew the surface of her morning beverage, and before taking a sip, asked, "Where are we?"

"Still in the ditch. Heading east toward the Apalachicola Bay and Carrabelle."

"How far is that?"

"It's quite a way."

They stayed together on deck, quiet but thinking practically the same thing: How does she get off this damn boat?

When she finished her coffee, Bill smiled. "I told you to make yourself at home. I'm sure you're a little hungry. There is plenty to eat in the fridge. Fix yourself something."

She did and left him to pilot the boat. He had the girl buzzing along. They were making four-and-a-half knots over the ground with the favorable current. Much later, a long straight canal appeared to starboard. Bill glanced and expanded the plotter. It was the cut to St. Joseph Bay. He shrunk the screen back to normal and dismissed it. It was never part of the plan. Fifteen or so minutes later, Carla came topside to join him. She was now back in her bikini top, and a black, very see-through sarong wrapped around her waist. As they stood there looking forward, a fixed bridge came into view. He checked the chart. White City. Underneath the bridge was a park and a boat ramp along with a dock along the channel to tie up to. *Perfect*, he thought. He turned to Carla. "We're going to stop here for a while. I have a short conference call in thirty minutes, so, if I had to guess, this place is probably as good as any."

She nodded her head as she was looking at her phone.

Genuinely concerned about her well-being, he asked, "Are you doing okay?"

She smiled. "I think so. I like it here."

"Good. Will you go forward and help me get her tied up?"

"Sure."

As he turned the boat in the channel to slow and come alongside, Bill noticed an older man near the dock, walking a little dog. As soon as the guy saw Carla, he eagerly moved in for a better look.

"Hey, Mate," Bill called out. "Do you mind taking a line?"

The guy clapped his hands together to indicate he was ready. "Carla... toss the line to him."

She did, and Bill scurried down and aft to feed the guy with a stern line.

"I appreciate your help, mate. Could have done it myself, but I'll never turn down a hand."

When the guy finished tying off the cleat, he stood and spoke to his little dog. "Bob's your uncle, Cressy. Now, there are two blokes in White City."

Bill said, "You're British!"

"And it's a beautiful morning, yeah?"

"Bloody beautiful. The name is Bill. Bring your little dog and come aboard."

The guy picked up his little dog, came aboard, and extended a hand. "The name is Danny. I live here in White City. Just had old Cressy here out for a little stroll."

Bill said, "I really do appreciate your help. Thanks again. Can I get you a cider?"

Danny said, "Not a problem, and yes," but his eyes ignored Bill. Carla was approaching. He moved past Bill, reaching out his hand to meet her. She took his fingers. "And who do we have here, Bill? Were you not going to introduce me?"

Bill chuckled at his enthusiasm. "Danny, this is Carla. She is a... good friend. Just along for the ride."

Danny turned toward Bill with raised eyebrows. "Just a friend, you say. Well, isn't that a bloody shame for you?"

Carla gave a little blush. "Aren't you the sweetest? And who do we have here?" She reached over to pet the dog.

"This is my Cressy. We live just down the street." He pointed under the bridge. "Just a few hundred meters that way."

Bill came back with two bottles of Strongbow and handed one to Danny. They clanked necks, and Bill said, "I have a scheduled call in a few minutes. It shouldn't take long. Please stay and keep Carla company. When I get done, you can join us for lunch. What do you say?"

He looked at Carla. "Oh, it would be my pleasure to keep your friend entertained."

Danny and Carla made time out on the aft deck. Chatting and getting on. Danny was several years older than Bill, and significantly older than Carla, but that didn't stop his flirting and carrying on. She divided her time between Danny and her phone, but she wasn't bored. And she would be lying if she said she didn't enjoy the attention. She especially found the stories of his friendship with the late Margaret Thatcher interesting and entertaining.

Inside the cabin, the call was wrapping up. It wasn't supposed to last more than fifteen minutes or so. It was just a chance for each of the teams in Chicago to go around the table and brief Bill on their progress. As the last brief concluded, Bill thanked everybody for all their hard work. Then he said, "And I would like to make a surprise announcement. Jerry? You're still on the line, right?"

"Sure, boss. I'm here."

"Good. Good. Folks, please join me in congratulating Jerry on his latest promotion."

Everybody around the Chicago conference table looked at Jerry. Jerry returned their gaze with the same level of confusion and surprise, then leaned toward the big speaker phone and said, "Well, thanks, Bill. I don't know what to say. I didn't see this coming."

Everyone in the room had their eyes on the tabletop speaker waiting for more details, none more than Jerry.

"Jerry, folks, will soon be heading up our international marketing team. It's a promotion long time coming."

People in the room cheered and gathered around Jerry to pat him on the back.

Jerry leaned closer to the speaker. "Damn, boss. Wow! What a surprise! I didn't see that coming."

"Neither did I, Jerry, until around nine-thirty last night. I know you'll do well and enjoy New Delhi."

The smile on Jerry's face retreated. "What did you just say, boss?"

"I said that I know that you will do a fine job."

"No, boss. The other part."

"Oh, about you enjoying India? You're going to love it. The office there is expecting you to report in by the end of November... Okay then, if there is nothing else gang, have a wonderful day." Bill ended the call.

Two minutes later, Bill's cell phone rang. "What is it, Jerry?"

"India? New Delhi? You are kidding, right? You're not serious."

"Did I sound like I was kidding? Congratulations."

"But I don't want to go to damn India."

"That's too bad. That's where I need you, and oh... by the way, you'll be happy to know they have Tinder there, too. Goodbye, Jerry." He ended the call with a smile.

Minutes later, he joined Carla and Danny with fresh ciders and a strong vodka and cranberry. They sat there for a while, and Carla excused herself to go for a walk.

When she was out of earshot, Danny said, "Mate, she smells of hormones and sex. I can't believe that you two..."

Bill raised his hand. "You are confusing hormones and sex with the looney tunes. She's batshit crazy."

"I like them a little crazy."

They sat, chatted, and got to know each other a little better. It was good to have someone from their mother country to talk with. As they became more familiar with one another, they watched Carla as she paced the park. After a while, Bill said, "Danny... I know we just met. I know you don't know me from Adam's cat. But... I need a huge favor."

"What?"

"If it wouldn't be too much trouble, and I'll pay for everything, could you get her off my boat and drive her home to Panama City? She's driving me bonkers."

Danny smiled as he watched her little butt swing back and forth. "Consider it done."

"Really? Oh, Mate, I'll owe you big."

"Bloody hell. I owe you!"

They both laughed and about the time they stopped, a new Corvette came racing around the corner. It slowed, then sped up when the driver saw Carla standing at the boat. The Vette slid to a stop. Carla and the driver were looking at their phones. Bill heard Carla say, "You must be Marcus."

The driver nodded his head.

"Hold on, I'll be right back."

Carla ran back on board and went inside the cabin. In short order, she came out and jumped on the dock. Then she stopped and walked aft so she could talk to Bill. "I'm sorry that it didn't work out."

"I'm sorry, too, but we both knew..."

She said, "Nothing's permanent."

"No, it's not."

With that, she turned around, ran to the Corvette, jumped in, and a trail of dust followed them out of the park and toward the bridge. And that is how Bill came to make a new friend who would later affectionately be known as Naked Danny.

18

CARRABELLE, FLORIDA

Think or Swim metaphorically chugged along across Wimico Lake and connected to the Apalachicola River and ultimately the bay. He never gave the idea of stopping in Apalach a thought, much less a second. He continued with one goal. Get to Carrabelle. To play it safe, he stayed in the channel hugging the inside shore of St. George Island. After clearing the Highway 300 bridge, two things happened. For one, the winds and the sea state were getting rough. It was directly on the nose, and the stronger the wind blew, the rougher the seas got, and the slower Bill's boat made headway. Things were getting tough and with the engines wide open, he was doing good to make one knot of speed over the ground. The weather never let up. Concerned with the distance left and the possibility or, more likely, the probability that things would get worse before they got better, he scanned the charts for a place to duck and hide. Rattlesnake Cove looked to be the answer. It was tricky navigating, but once he cleared the point and got behind the lee of the shore, life got better. After getting the hook down and set, he went to the galley for a cider. Before trying to take a sip, he realized he was still panting from the excitement. Once he got a good swallow down, he was thankful for two things: that he and his boat were now safe and that batshit crazy Carla hadn't been aboard. Now that he was safe, imagining how she would have come unglued gave him a good laugh, but in the heat and stress of the moment... it wouldn't have been funny at all.

When he went to bed, the wind was still howling, but when he woke up the next morning, the front had pushed through; the air was still, and the seas were flat. He entered the Carrabelle River and made it to town without issue. What a difference. The day before he battled a raging windstorm and choppy seas, today was effortless with *Think or Swim* cutting through pacified waters.

The experience had taught him one thing though: taking his boat out into the open Gulf of Mexico and across to the next leg of the ICW could be a tricky and potentially unwise without a favorable and extended weather window. And he thought about it every day, because the day after his arrival, the winds kicked up again. Waking up each morning to find all the local flags standing at attention served as a daily reminder that *today would not be the day*.

It was now November and the subtle weather shift meant more of the same. Cooler temps and steady winds coming out of the north. He felt trapped, and, to make matters worse, he didn't find Carrabelle all that appealing. It certainly wasn't the place where he wanted his journey to end. After three and a half weeks of sitting around waiting, he wondered if he would ever get out of there.

One afternoon, after drinking his last Strongbow cider, he picked up his phone and scrolled through his contact list. Then he found what he was looking for, The Governor of White City. He hit dial. When the familiar British accent answered, Bill said, "Danny. I'm out of Strongbow, dammit. And this bloody town doesn't carry it?"

"Where are you, mate?"

"Carrabelle."

"I thought you'd be further on down the line by now."

"It's been the weather. It has me a bit cheesed off. Can't get a string of days when the wind isn't a problem."

"But you're out of cider, yeah?"

"Yeah."

"We can't have that. I'm on my way. Where are you tied up at?"

Bill told him, but said, "You don't have to do that, mate. I just called to chat."

"Ah, balderdash. Just got up from a little kip and need something to do. I'll head that way now. Be there in a jiffy. We'll get the knees up and get a little pissed."

"Are you sure?"

There was no answer. Danny had already hung up.

Two hours later, Danny and Cressy were coming down the dock. Danny carried two cases of cider. When he got to the boat, he looked up at Bill and said, "There are three more cases in the back seat."

Danny was good company for Bill. And Bill turned out to be the same for Danny. Sometimes you long for some company from the homeland. Bill cooked steaks on the grill and they got plenty sloshed on cider. Plus, they got to know each other much better. When Bill mentioned his anxiety about crossing the gulf alone, Danny provided the perfect solution.

"I'd cross with you, but why in the hell would you want to, anyway?"

"Well," said Bill, "I don't like it here and I need to move on."

"But you have already passed the best part of Florida. You didn't even stop?"

"Where?"

"Port St. Joe. You just cruised on by. In the morning, we'll drive over, and Cressy and I will show you around. You'll love it. There is nothing posh about it, but that's the best part."

"Are you sure?"

"Beats the bugger all you do around here every day."

The next day, it took Bill only ten minutes to see the whole town. When the big tour was over, he thought about it for ten seconds more. Then he looked at his new mate and said, "Take me back by the marina."

Danny smiled and Bill found Port St. Joe.

19

TALK TO MICHAEL

The months and seasons rolled on, and life was good for Charlene. She had found a niche group of ladies from the shop that she worked with and others from around town. They all made for good company, and they supported each other when one or more of the husbands had become a pain in the ass. They had become a tight group, and you rarely saw one without one or more being close by.

There's Lydia, Aubrey, Sadie, Donna, Peyton, and Cora.

All seven ladies have much in common: a love of music, good southern cooking, and some form of alcohol. From vodka to chardonnay. The only big difference being, the other gals had husbands. Charlene had Zoey.

Only once at the marina, during a late summer Dockside Café sunset and wine session, did one of the gals in the posse try to play matchmaker.

The ladies sat tall in their high-back Adirondacks, looking out over the boats toward the horizon. Their phones were ready, prepared to add to the hundreds of sunset pictures already hogging up space on their memory cards.

"Charlene. There is this new guy in town. I really think you would like him. Maybe..."

"Lydia... what are you talking about?"

"A fella, Charlene. Nice guy and good-looking. We could have y'all over..."

Charlene raised her phone in the air. "I can't hear you now. Sorry."

The other gals laughed.

Lydia gave a little huff and raised her voice. "I said..."

"Shut up, Lydia. Just stop. I know you mean well. But we've all talked about this before and the consensus was we wouldn't talk about it. Ever."

"I know, but..."

"But nothing."

Sadie changed the subject. "There it goes, ladies. It's dropping fast."

Click, click, click, click...

And as quickly as the sun dropped, so did the idea of trying to hook up Charlene with some man.

Later that night, Charlene sat up in her bed, replaying the day. It played out much like it did in Tennessee when her friend Betty wanted to play matchmaker. Back then, Charlene spoke the truth, but things were different now. She would never admit it to her girlfriends. She couldn't stand the idea of them having pity on her. But she was tired of being by herself. She wasn't getting any younger and the thought of one day dying alone scared her. Tears filled her eyes, but what scared her even more made her dry those tears away. Settling. Regardless of how lonely it might get; Charlene couldn't stomach the idea of settling for just a man.

I couldn't stand the idea... hell, I wouldn't stand for the idea. She deserves better than to settle. I just wouldn't let that happen if I could avoid it. Then she prayed, and it blew me away. I never saw it coming. Well... I did, but it was how she prayed.

"Oh, Lord. Please. I am done being alone." She gave a little giggle. "Zoey needs a father figure around here." Then her face turned sad and tired. The tears returned. "Please, God, help me. Place a good man in my life. I'm not interested in my friends trying to help. We've been down that road before. No... I want you to help, because if you do, I'll know it would be heaven-sent and meant to be." She was quiet for a spell as she rocked back and forth. She clasped her hands together and said, "Lord, go find my husband, Michael. He knows. Michael will show you what kind of man I need, because if I can't have him, I need one just as good or the next best thing. Amen."

20

THE DRUNK DONKEY

It was the sixth of October 2018. It was warm, dry, and pleasant. Tourist season had certainly slowed down, though a few stragglers showed up for the Columbus Day weekend. Area locals were in a festive mood. Many from Port St. Joe ventured over to Apalachicola for the annual Octoberfest celebration held at Oyster City Brewing. It is an all-day event full of friendly folks, great music, and fantastic beer. Oyster City wasn't around when I was still alive, but I can tell. I would have loved it.

Many of Charlene's tribe had gone to Apalach, and she probably would have gone too, had she not had to work at the boutique. She didn't mind, though. Once she closed the shop, she would head home, pick up Zoey, and meet Sadie at the marina for wine and a sunset. Sadie had to work, too.

The weather was gorgeous. So gorgeous that nobody paid attention to the weathermen and their casual mentioning of the tropical disturbance down around the Yucatan Peninsula.

The tone of weathermen changed the next morning when they upgraded the storm twice; first in the early hours to a tropical depression, then Tropical Storm Michael was born. When the storm grew into a hurricane the next morning, it got a lot of chatter on the news wire. Even so, folks on the Gulf

Coast are used to this. Hurricanes, cones of uncertainty, and most likely a landfall that would not affect them. Even as the cone narrowed, people shrugged their shoulders. Until there is something to worry about, why waste the effort?

On that Monday, Charlene was at work. The store opened at 10:00 and Oyster Radio was reporting on the storm. Many local jurisdictions had already issued voluntary evacuation orders. At 11:00, Charlene's phone dinged with a notification. She ignored it.

Dang it. I snuck up behind her and said, "Check it, dammit."

She turned around. "What did you say?" she asked.

The other girl working said, "I didn't say anything, Charlene. Are you hearing things?"

Charlene chuckled as she reached for her phone. "I guess I'm going crazy."

It had been a Facebook notification that Mike's Weather Page was about to go live.

She opened the app. Moments later, Mike went live. "Hey, everybody. It's your Drunk Donkey here. Boy, do we have some things to go over. Tropical Storm Michael wasted no time. Folks, he's a hurricane now."

Mike paused a bit, and Charlene saw something on his face. Then she heard it in his voice.

"I don't know folks. I think the National Hurricane Center has underplayed this one. It could be a problem."

Charlene looked up at the other girls and the owner. "Hey, y'all. Come listen."

They gathered around.

"Just yesterday, they, the NHC, advised that this thing *could...*" He used his fingers to make air quotes. "...be a hurricane by Wednesday. Well, surprise! It is two days out, and he is already showing his teeth."

The ladies gathered around with even more interest as he explained much of what Ted had briefed at the NHC. The conditions were perfect for the creation of a monster. Then he pulled up the screen of all the various landfall models. They had tightened some, which narrowed the cone of uncertainty. But then he took a long drink and said, "I don't know folks, if I had to guess, you folks right here better take cover." With his mouse, he painted a line along the coast from Panama City to Indian Pass.

The ladies raised their heads and looked at each other.

"What do you think?" asked one girl.

Charlene says, "I think we should take this one seriously."

Seconds later, as they stood there, Oyster Radio announced that Gulf County upgraded the coastal voluntary evacuations to mandatory.

Moments after that, they turned off the open sign, locked the door, and scurried to get the shop ready for whatever came.

21

For two days, the Port St. Joe Marina and the public boat ramp were a flurry of activity. On Monday, many couldn't wait to get out of town. Those with trailers left their wet slips and pulled their boats for higher ground. It was steady traffic. On that Tuesday, the remaining boats, too big to pull out, got underway for the Saul Creek anchorage. A favorite hurricane hole between Lake Wimico and Apalachicola.

One of the fishing guides was about to shove off when he stopped and spoke with Bill. "You need to get out of here. Saul Creek will be crowded, but find a spot to tuck away in on the ICW. Ya hear me, now? Things might get ugly."

Bill nodded, and as he looked around at all hustle and bustle, he saw Danny walking down the dock. Bill walked to meet him. "Morning, Danny."

"You need to get out of here, mate."

"That seems to be the recommended advice, but where? I was told Saul Creek would be full, not that I even know where that is."

"Come on," said Danny. "Cast off, we'll find a spot. Maybe there will be a spot open in the oxbow at Clay or Searcy Creek."

Off they went.

When they got to White City, Danny grabbed his boat and

followed along.

From the time they left the marina, it took over three-and-a-half hours to make it to the oxbow at Clay Creek. Two large fishing boats were already there. There was room for one more. Bill picked his spot, dropped the anchor, and put out a hundred feet of chain rode as he backed in toward a big stand of cypress trees. After tying off and securing *Think or Swim* to the trees, Bill and Danny sat down for a couple of ciders. When they finished, Danny stood, shook Bill's hand, wished him luck, then dashed away back to White City. He, too, had to prep and evacuate in his RV.

Bill, along with two others, were left alone to ride out the storm.

***

The night before, Charlene had packed her bags and put them in the car. Her evacuation plan was to visit Madelyn and Ophelia in Tennessee. But... that wasn't my plan for her.

When her alarm went off, she hit snooze. Still exhausted from securing the shop, she wanted a few more minutes of sleep. Zoey wouldn't have anything to do with it. Stinky breath and gentle kisses brought Charlene around.

"Oh, Zoey! Let me be for a minute."

She didn't. Zoey knew it was time to get the hell out of Dodge.

On Zoey's third round of kisses, Charlene sat up. "Okay, okay, Ohhhhh my God, that hurts."

I gritted my teeth. "Sorry, Charlie."

"Oh, my back! My God. What did I do?"

Okay, let me be clear here. She overdid it at the boutique.

Spending the day lifting and slinging those boxes and getting merchandise off the floor to higher ground took its toll. I just helped make it seem worse. Okay, okay. Call me a bastard. That's fair, but I have a plan here.

Despite her discomfort, she was still damned and determined to go to Tennessee. I couldn't let that happen. By the time she got to Dothan, Alabama, the pain was more than she could handle. She could barely get out of the car to top off the fuel tank. That's when she knew. She would never make it to Tennessee. Feeling defeated, she called her other sister, Sarah, only 40 miles away in Donalsonville.

Sarah saw Charlene's name on the screen. "Hey, Charlene. How are you coming along?"

"Not worth a damn. I'm headed your way."

"I thought you were headed north?"

"I'll never make it. Pulled something in my back. I'm gonna stay with you and Ethan, if that is okay."

"Of course it is. Where are you?"

"Just east of Dothan. I'll be there in about thirty minutes. That is, if...Ohhhhh, damn... I don't need an ambulance first."

Donalsonville is about two hours from the coast, so during a hurricane threat, it is understandable that the level of urgency and need for preparedness isn't on equal footing as it is by the shore. If it comes their way, it will be more of a nuisance than anything. One can reasonably expect a few trees to go down, and losing power is certainly possible. The biggest threat of an inland hurricane is tornadoes. Either way, once a hurricane makes landfall, it deteriorates and weakens quickly.

Sarah runs the local nursing home in town. And with Michael looking more and more like he would pass through the area, she had to remain on station to make sure her residents were safe. When Sarah's husband got home from work, the house smelled great. He found Charlene in the kitchen. Every eye on the stove had a pot on it. The oven was cooking a smorgasbord of meats.

"Charlene! What the hell are you doing?"

"Hush up, Ethan. I'm a nervous wreck. Have you not been watching the forecast?"

"No. Not really. I've been at work."

"Well, they say it will be at least a Category 4 now. At least! Maybe more."

"Okay, Charlene. That's fine, but do you have to cook everything in the house?"

Charlene spun around and put her hands on her hips. "I cook, Ethan. That's what I do when I get like this. And when we lose power, you'll bc damn glad to have something to eat."

22

October 10, 2018: Landfall

The Florida Panhandle woke up as a bullseye for Michael, now a high-end Category 4 hurricane. Heavy wind bands, torrential rain, and vicious surf pounded the shoreline, and the storm's eye was still four to five hours away. The worst was yet to come. It had grown into a massive destructive system that continued to intensify. And not too long before the last hurricane-hunting plane exited the maelstrom, Michael kicked up his heels to Category 5 with sustained winds of over 160 miles per hour. The strongest storm to hit the Panhandle.

Two hours before its estimated landfall, the NWS in Tallahassee issued its first-ever Excessive Wind Warning (EWW) for Bay, Gulf, and Franklin counties. The assessment of the storm by analysts showed it continued to intensify during landfall, causing the NWS to extend the EWWs well into the rest of North Florida and into Alabama and Georgia.

The next several hours proved devastating for nearly everything in Michael's path. The most damage stretched from Panama City to Indian Pass, and while the destruction from the storm was extensive, the full wrath of Michael fell upon the small town of Mexico Beach. The eye of the storm came ashore on the far eastern side of Tyndall Air Force. This placed the eastern side of the eye, the most powerful part of any hurricane, on the shores of that quiet, beloved seaside town. Mexico Beach had been a favorite, family-friendly vacation spot for many decades. Its charm came from all the old and quaint beach houses and cottages that served the holiday needs of beachgoers for generations.

However, on that dreadful day, Michael took it all away. Virtually everything was swept away, gone. Like it never existed.

The high winds and storm surge could be felt as far as Apalachicola. Of those that refused to evacuate, many would later admit that they would never do that again. As terrifying as it was, it paled compared to what the skippers and crews went through as they fought to keep their vessels and livelihoods afloat on Saul Creck. That included Bill and the two other skippers that struggled in a small, protected oxbow on the ICW just west of Searcy Creek.

As they waited for the worst, they spoke regularly on the radio. Jim operated the larger dual-engine center console, while Bobby did his best to keep his single-engine boat from peril. But once things got ugly, there was no time for casual chit-chat.

While they were about twenty miles to the east of the eye, they were on the wrong side of destiny, not that they had much choice. The adage, when it comes to hurricanes, that *West is best* holds true. The eastern side of the storm, with its counterclockwise motion, brings not only onshore winds but the dangers of the flooding surge. The combination of the two creates the most damage in any hurricane. The winds and waters that were rising and cutting through Cape San Blas and Port St. Joe greeted them with a healthy slap. Survival mode set in.

For the next several hours, total chaos engulfed them. As the waters rose and the wind howled, lines stretched, and anchors dragged. The restraints that contained them needed constant attention and adjustments, a hard thing to do when the wind makes it nearly impossible to stand or walk and the sideways rain feels like needles against your skin.

Think or Swim was the largest of the three. She also carried the most windage. Her broad, exposed sides caused her to lean over violently in the heavy gusts, popping back up-right when the pressure eased. Luckily, her plow anchor did a fair job of holding... most of the time. Plus, Bill and Danny had tied up to cypress trees. The other two had tied to oaks, and the combination of the surging flood and wind pulled the roots free of the ground. They were now adrift and had to fight to free themselves of lines and catastrophe. One tree hit *Think or Swim* as it floated by and luckily caused no damage.

The water was up by at least nine feet. They were in the thick of it. Bob and his boat did their best but couldn't overpower the forces of the wind. Bill and Jim watched in horror as Bob was being carried deeper and deeper into the woods and treetops.

Jim's boat, with her enormous engines, could better manage the conditions. With the smaller boat heading for certain disaster, Jim sprang into action and went to his aid. Bill watched as Jim, obviously a seasoned skipper, skillfully maneuvered into the treetops, cast a line to Bob, and pulled him free from peril. All in the middle of the storm. For whatever reason, Bob couldn't restart his engine and Jim had no choice but to tow Bob to safety. There was only one logical destination, so they headed east, away from the storm and toward Apalachicola. They all three maintained radio communication for a while, until the range between them became too great. Bill was now alone to weather what was left of the storm.

***

The decision to extend the EWWs into Alabama and Georgia was prudent. Though nobody had ever heard of such, it left them totally unprepared, not knowing what to expect. Such a warning was unchartered territory. They were about to find out what an EWW stands for.

After landfall, Michael made his turn to the northeast and weaved his destructive way through the towns of Marianna and Blountstown as a Cat 4, picking apart just about everything he touched. The vast stretches of timberland that make up a good portion of the panhandle were not spared. He destroyed it all in one afternoon. All that remained were pine stumps that reached thirty to forty feet in the air. It was as if Michael took a chainsaw, and, from one side of the storm to the other, cut the valuable timber in half. Big oaks were pushed over and set aside like they were just in the way. As he passed over I-10, he left a debris field that closed the Interstate in both directions through the next day. The destruction was mindboggling.

Lower Alabama's and southern Georgia's proximity to the coast often gets to feel the extreme effects of hurricanes that make a Panhandle landfall. But this was different. When Michael entered Georgia and reached Bainbridge and Donalsonville, he held on to his strength with all he could muster and remained a Category 3 hurricane. Just as in the Panhandle towns in Florida, they were left crippled and without power.

As the storm raged on, Charlene was a nervous wreck. Not

just because of the weather war that raged outside, but because her brother-in-law kept going outside to watch the storm.

"Ethan! Get your butt back in this house."

"Charlene, did you see that? The old, massive oak across the street was uprooted and thrown on its side."

"I don't care about that. Just get in here."

He came in and slammed the door. "This is going to be one hell of a mess."

The power had been ripped out of service for more than an hour. Charlene spoke to her sister on the phone once, and she seemed to be safe. But then, in a blink of an eye, cell service was gone. The towers had been stripped of their antennas. It was a scary time as she worried about her sibling, but she knew the nursing home was built like a fort and that comforted her.

Once the storm had passed, and the winds had fallen to tropical storm levels, people emerged to survey the damage. Ethan was one of the first.

"Stay here, Charlene. I'm going to check on your sister. I'll only be a few minutes."

A while later, he returned and reported that Sarah and the rest of the residents were fine. A numbing stare stretched across his face.

"How bad is it?"

"Roads are impassable. Trees down everywhere over the roads. Will you do me a favor? Put some food together while I load the chainsaws up in the truck. Me and the boys got to clear some of these trees. There's nobody else to do it."

She did, and she sent him with enough grub to feed a small army. Plus, she added three of the several one-gallon jugs of spring water they had bought to prepare for the storm.

He thanked her, kissed her on the cheek, and said, "I'm going to be gone for a bit."

Charlene was exhausted. The lack of sleep the night before, coupled with the emotional strain and worry caused by the storm, had her running on adrenaline. As the juice that kept her going backed away, she and Zoey collapsed on the sofa. She closed her eyes. As the sound of the wind continued to subside, it was replaced by the buzzing and screaming of more than a hundred chainsaws as they ripped through pine and oak.

23

THE DAY AFTER

B ill wasn't sure when he finally crashed, but he remembered two things; not to let himself go to bed until he was sure the worst was over, and that he had never felt more exhausted in his life.

When he opened his eyes, the quiet had an eerie feeling. The boat was perfectly still as she rode at anchor. When he emerged on deck, the sun was just coming up, and the waters had receded and looked like glass. The surrounding trees reflected on the water like a mirror. Now and then, baitfish snapped at bugs on the surface, disrupting the calm. The stillness was beautiful. Twelve hours earlier, he was in the middle of Hell, but now he rested on the backwaters of paradise.

The knots used to tie off at the trees had endured so much strain and pressure that they were impossible to untie. They had welded themselves together and had to be cut free.

The plow anchor did its job and dug in deep. It took a while to break free, but the anchor windlass finally did its job and got it out of and off the bottom. Before long, he was free and headed back toward White City. The ride back through the ditch was peaceful. It was hard to imagine that a monstrous storm had come through the day before. That all changed once he got to White City.

As Bill approached the docks, a heavily damaged shrimp boat was tied up, listing something awful to port. She was taking on water and her skipper worked frantically to get the gas-powered pump running to get ahead of the leak and the incoming water. Bill offered his help and within a few minutes, the pump was running.

As he stood and took in the surroundings, he thought of Danny. He headed to his place, climbing through and over fallen trees to check on him, but he wasn't there. Neither was his RV. He had obviously evacuated. Once Bill got back to the White City docks, he fumbled for the keys to his car, which he and Danny had previously staged under the bridge. *Had it flooded? Would it even start?*

To his surprise, it did, and off he went to check on Port St. Joe and his slip at the marina. He found the town a colossal mess. Boats and debris were everywhere. Many were piled up in the Piggly Wiggly parking lot, others were scattered like litter on the other side of Highway 98. When he drove down Marina Drive and saw the damage, he couldn't believe his eyes. It was gone, nearly all of it. All that remained were a few sailboats thrown up on what remained of the docks, and fewer still banged up and floating in their slips or adrift. Several boats were high and dry on the marina grounds. He got back in his car to drive back to his boat, knowing one thing. He wouldn't be coming back.

***

When Charlene woke up the next morning, she and Zoey were alone. The sounds of chainsaws continued to echo in the distance. At some point, Ethan came in during the night.

The bag of food she had given him, now empty, sat on the kitchen counter. She walked outside, and all the sawdust from the cleanup gave the air the clean smell of freshly cut pine and oak. Then she saw her car and knew she had to get back to St. Joe.

She threw together a few things to snack on, a box of red wine, and her personal bag. She stepped out the door with Zoey and looked around. "Come on, Zoey. We got to get home."

There are only so many ways to get to Port. St. Joe from Donalsonville, but plenty of trees along the way. Getting to St. Joe that morning was a struggle, but where trees had once blocked the road, they were now cut away to make room for traffic. In some places, just enough for one lane of traffic. And if the good old boys weren't done making a hole in the road, she waited patiently. What would normally be a two-hour drive took over three and a half. Once she arrived at the ICW bridge at White City, she was met by blue lights and a Gulf County deputy. She rolled down the window.

"Morning, ma'am. Sorry, the bridge is closed."

"Oh... is it damaged?"

"No, Ma.am. We're not letting anybody into St. Joe while the initial cleanup is still going on."

"How long will it be closed?"

"Not, sure. Probably through the night. And then, just people with genuine business will be let back in. Do you live in town?"

"Yes."

"Then it shouldn't be a problem."

She looked away. "What am I going to do?"

Her words weren't for the deputy. She was just thinking out loud. But he didn't realize that.

"They have set up a shelter in the high school gym back in Wewa. You could go there if you have nowhere else to go."

There was no way she was going to a shelter. That wasn't even going to happen. She looked around to think.

"Could I go under the bridge and stay down in the park?"

"Ma'am... that is entirely up to you."

***

When Bill descended the bridge back toward White City, a deputy was just setting up the roadblock. When the officer saw Bill coming down the ramp, he waved him down. Bill slowed to a stop and rolled down his window.

"Sir, if you have good reason to return to St. Joe, turn around and go back now. Once you leave, I can't let you back in until it is clear."

Bill sat there, thinking for a few seconds. Fond memories of the last several months in St. Joe rushed through his head. It brought on a somberness and a realization that nothing ever lasts. He looked up at the deputy and said, "Thank you very much, but no... I'm afraid I won't ever be coming back."

The deputy tipped his hat. "Then safe travels, sir." Then he gestured to Bill to proceed.

From inside *Think or Swim*, Bill watched the shrimp boat slowly right itself as water splashed into the ICW from the pump. The shrimper walked around on deck, so Bill went to check on him.

As he approached, the shrimper said, "Thanks for your help earlier."

"Not a problem, but I did nothing. You would have gotten the pump going, eventually. I just helped tinker with it."

"Well, I appreciate the *tinkering*."

"No worries. Did you find the leak?"

"Found two. A thru-hull fitting had lost its seal and water was getting past quite steady like. Plus, the prop shaft took a beating last night when we got caught up in another boat's anchor chain. The stuffing box is shot. Lots of water getting in there, especially when the screw is turning."

"If there's anything I can do, I'll be over on my boat."

As Bill walked back to *Think or Swim*, he noticed a lone vehicle parked by one of the small, sheltered picnic tables.

Charlene had Zoey in her lap and her nose in her phone. She never noticed the man that casually passed by to investigate.

Of course, they had never met, but Bill observed her in a car full of stuff and all the windows down. She didn't seem to be in much distress, so he passed back by on the way to his boat. Halfway there, he stopped and turned to look at her. She still hadn't noticed him, and he walked back toward her.

The last thing he wanted to be was threatening, so he approached from the passenger side window and from a safe distance back stooped down. "Miss?"

Charlene did a little jump behind the wheel. "Oh, you gave me a start."

"I'm sorry, Miss. I was just wondering. Are you okay?"

"I would be if this darn phone would work. Nobody knows where I am."

"You can forget it. Cell service is down. Probably it will be for a while. What are you doing here?"

"They won't let me cross the bridge. I live in Port St. Joe, so I'm going to stay in my car until the morning when they will let me."

"Stay in your car? Sleep... here?"

"I don't have much choice."

Bill studied her for a bit and thought, *I must be crazy.* Then he said, "Sure you do."

"What do you mean?"

"You don't have to sleep in your car. You can stay on my boat till the morning."

"What boat?"

Bill pointed.

Charlene looked at the big Carver and thought about it. All the scenarios raced through her brain. The last one was the worst possible and a look of terror showed on her face.

With a sincere smile, Bill said, "I can promise you. I'm not a murderer. You'll live to see the morning."

Still looking concerned, she said, "I'm sure that's what Ted Bundy used to say."

"Who?"

"Forget it."

"Really. I promise. You will be safe on my boat, but can you make the same promise?"

"What?"

"Are you a murderer?"

That made Charlene laugh.

"I didn't think so, but I had to ask."

"But I have my dog?"

"Your dog is welcome too."

Charlene contemplated her options.

Once again, I whispered in her ear. "Go to the boat, Charlie. Don't be an idiot."

Charlene shook her head in surprise. "What did you say?"

Bill shook his head. "I said 'the dog was welcome too.'"

"No... after that."

Bill shook his head. "What did you hear?"

As Charlene shook her head and thought, *He'll think I'm*

crazy, he thought, *This one might be bloody mental, too.*

She continued to ponder. It could be just as dangerous to stay in the car all night. There would be people desperate enough to kill her for what little she had. Whether they would find her, alone and helpless, in the car was the question. She glanced back at the boat and thought, *He doesn't look all that desperate.* She made a comparison. *If I had to die tonight, would I rather die in my car or on a nice boat? Huh!*

"Well," she said, "if you're sure?"

He smiled. "I am very sure, I think. Let me help you with your things."

With their arms loaded with stuff from the car, they headed to the boat. When they got there, Bill put his things down to help Charlene climb aboard. Charlene put her things down too and stuck out her hand. "I'm Charlene Jones."

Bill gently took her hand. "My name is Bill Salisbury. I'm pleased to meet you."

"Me too," said Charlene. As he helped her and Zoey on the boat, she added, "I think."

24

WELCOME TO "THINK OR SWIM"

B ill gestured toward the salon. "Make yourself at home and get comfortable, then I'll give you the quick tour."

As Bill dashed away to make sure the head was in order, the first thing Charlene noticed was the air conditioning. *Oh, my.*

He showed her around the boat, not that it took very long.

She put her hands on her hips. "Where are you from?"

He liked her southern, country girl accent. Smiling, he said, "The middle of England, outside of Manchester. I grew up on a farm there."

She liked his English accent, too. "And what is it with all the solar panels?"

He laughed and told her his story. After he finished, he expected the same. "So, tell me about Charlene Jones."

"Well," she started, "there isn't much to tell."

But in classic Charlene style, she found plenty to tell him, and he didn't mind listening.

After a while, Bill looked at his watch. It was well into the afternoon. They had talked the day away. "Oh, dear. Look at the time and we've had nothing to eat. Are you hungry?"

Charlene looked at her watch. "Oh, my. Now that you mention it, yes. Let me see what I have."

"Check the pantry, too. I have some things in there as well."

Charlene went through her food and said, "How does cheese and crackers sound?"

"Sounds delicious."

Charlene held up her box of wine. "And I brought some of the finest. Would you like a glass? I hear it was a very good month?"

They laughed, and Bill suggested they get comfortable and eat outside on the back of the boat. They sat with their table of hors d'oeuvres between them and the box of red wine close at hand. They nibbled away and enjoyed the conversation and the vino as the early evening approached.

After a while, an RV came around the corner from under the bridge. It steadied its course toward *Think or Swim*. Its tires locked up as the driver threw on the brakes and the long rolling camper slid to a stop. The driver got out and ran toward the boat. As he ran, he observed the goings-on at the boat's stern. His run was geared down to a jog. Then to a fast walk before stopping at the dock. "What in bloody hell is all this?"

"Hello, Danny. How do you mean?"

He waved his hands at Bill and Charlene. "I'm talking about... this!"

"Oh, Danny. Stop talking rubbish. Charlene, this is my friend Danny. He is the governor of White City. Danny, this is my friend Charlene Jones."

"You have wine! Wine! And what is that?" Danny craned his head to look. "Cheese and crackers! Oh, now isn't that just cheeky?"

Charlene laughed at the exchange.

"Danny, for crying out loud. Don't throw a wobble. Just come out with it."

"Okay, mate. I'll tell you. I've spent all day with folks cutting a path through downed trees, from Chipley through

Marianna, just so I could get back here and check the only other bloke I know. I've been worried sick that you might have drowned or something. But no! Here you are relaxed, living a posh life… And you have a woman on your boat. A woman!"

"Oh, tosh, my good man. Come to your senses."

Danny turned, flung his hands in the air, and walked back to his RV. "I'm absolutely knackered. I'm going home."

Bill smiled, and Charlene lightly chuckled as they watched Danny walk back to his RV. They could hear him grumbling all the way. "Wine… and a bloody woman. He's got a woman on the boat."

"That's my very best mate. He's a good friend."

"He seemed a bit upset. Will he be, okay?"

"Oh, yeah. He'll be fine. He's just lost the plot, that's all. Once he gets some rest, Bob's your uncle."

"Lost the plot?"

"Means he's not coping well. A little mental."

"Huh. You guys sure do talk funny."

Bill laughed and said, "You should hear yourself some time. More wine?"

As the sun was setting and they were cleaning up to go back inside, Bill's phone dinged with a notification.

"Was that your phone? They must have restored service," said Charlene.

Bill looked at his phone. "No. Still no service. That was an email."

"An email? An email without cell service?"

"Came through my Internet connection."

"Internet? We don't have cell service, but you have an Internet connection?"

"Yes, I must have it for my work. So, I have a large antenna that brings in AT&T."

"You're kidding me?"

Bill said nothing.

"You got electricity, you got running water and working toilets, you got refrigeration and air conditioning, and to top everything else... you got the Internet." Charlene laughed. "Well, if that don't beat all."

"How do you mean?"

"In one day, and for God knows how long, a storm left most people in this county and others with little to nothing to work with, but you still have everything. You are quite blessed." Charlene thought for a second, then continued, "And that makes me pretty blessed, too."

Bill smiled. "Let's go inside before the bugs feast on us."

They settled in the salon and had another glass of wine. They mostly talked about riding out the hurricane. After all, it really was the only thing they had in common. She spoke of how the storm ravaged her hometown, and with amazement, she listened to him describe riding out the storm on the boat. He often took videos, and they watched some clips on his television. It was all very scary and difficult for them both to relive.

When they were done talking about the storm, Charlene asked, "Can you get YouTube on the TV?"

Minutes later, she introduced Bill to the likes of Joe Bonamassa, Beth Hart, and J.J. Grey. They binged on the blues and other music for hours. During a J.J. Grey song, Charlene said, "This is a good one to dance to."

"We could. If you want to."

"What? Dance?"

"I'm not much of a dancer, but yeah."

So, they did, to the rest of the song. It wasn't a romantic dance, but it felt right at that moment in time. A pleasant distraction from what they had been through.

When the song was done, Bill said, "It's getting late. We should probably turn in. Will you and Zoey be alright here in the salon?"

"Yes, we will be just fine."

Bill got her a pillow and a blanket before heading down to his stateroom. When she heard him latch and lock the door, she giggled and said to her dog. "Zoey, I think he's more worried about us killing him than we are about him killing us."

***

The next morning, Charlene woke up first. Zoey was more than ready for a walk. She grabbed her cell phone and took the dog outside. As Zoey looked for a place to do her business, Charlene's eyes remained glued to the screen of her phone. Now and then, a bar would pop up. Not enough for a call, but perhaps a text. She typed out a group text to her sisters and Madelyn.

I hope y'all get this. Cell service not good yet. I'm okay. Waiting for the White City bridge to open. Stayed with a nice man on his boat last night. Zoey and I are fine. Don't worry.

She hit the send button.

It took a few minutes, but the message took flight.

A few seconds later, Madelyn's phone dinged. She was sitting around the kitchen table drinking coffee with her significant other. She grabbed her phone and read the message. "Well, son of a bitch." She typed a reply.

"What is it?"

Madelyn raised her hand. *Hold on. Let me finish*. She did, hit send, and put the phone down.

"What?" asked Spencer.

"Shit, Spencer... we were worried about momma, and last night she went and got on some damn houseboat or something with some strange man."

"You're kidding me?"

"No. I'm not."

"What did you tell her?"

"I just told he that she's crazy and not right in the brain." She shook her head. "She got on a *damn* boat with a stranger!"

Spencer chuckled. "Only your momma..."

When Charlene got back to the boat, Bill was making coffee. "Good morning," he said. "Coffee?"

"Please."

"Should be ready soon."

"They are going to let me in."

"What?"

"The bridge. We walked to the roadblock. Deputy said that since I live there and have property to manage, I could squeeze by."

"Well, that's good news."

"I hope so. Kind of scared to see what I'll find."

Bill nodded.

Once they were through with coffee, Charlene stood and announced, "I better get going. I can't put off the inevitable. What about you? Where are you going to go?"

"Not sure. I can't stay here for long. I may stick it out another day or so, then I guess I'll head west."

"Well, thank you again for letting us stay with you."

"Beats sleeping in the car."

Charlene gave him that big old smile. "Maybe just a little bit."

"Hold on. Before you go." He reached for a pad and paper

and jotted his name and number down. She did the same. "If the Post Office is open, would you buzz me or shoot a text to let me know? I have some things to mail later."

"Sure."

Bill helped her off the boat, watched her go to her car, then disappear around the corner. He shook his head. *That was crazy.*

25

NONE OF US ARE PERFECT

C harlene went straight to the property. She knew
Madelyn and Jolene would want a damage report. The
grounds were a mess, and there was roof damage, but the units
were dry. The flooding surge came close but never breached
the property line. That was a blessing in and of itself. Many
others were not as fortunate.

There was a hole in the roof from a fallen tree, so a good
amount of rainwater had gotten into the main unit. The
weather was clear, so she opened the windows to let the units
breathe. Then she jumped in the car to survey the area.

As she drove through town, she was awestruck at the
damage. Activity at the Piggly Wiggly caught her attention, so
she went to investigate. After driving through all the scattered
boats, she saw a line of folks out front. There was no backup
power for the store, so the grocery staff wasn't allowing anyone
inside. But they would take your limited list of items and shop
for you on a cash basis. It was a sad sight and painfully slow.
Her drive east out on Highway 98 was even sadder. The Port
Inn had taken a severe beating. Both the Exxon and Chevron
stations had been washed out and destroyed. There was no
telling when gas would be available again. She checked her
gauge, half a tank. *Better conserve.* Burger King was done too,

but that might be seen as a capital improvement. The Sunset Bar and Grill that sat directly on the bay took the full brunt of the storm. Its future couldn't be good. And the waterfront First United Methodist Church was going to need extensive repair.

She kept driving. All the older homes that faced the bay were washed out. It was all so sad. Not wanting to waste fuel, she circled back by Monument Avenue. She covered her mouth as she drove. It was much the same. Some homes had floated or were blown off their foundations, and those that had not were opened and their contents emptied and carried out to sea with the receding waters.

She watched people wander around what remained of their homes. They looked to be in a numb stupor, searching for anything that could be salvaged from what was left of their lives. Many others were in the street, talking and hugging their neighbors. She weaved her way through the residential streets to get to Long Avenue and found more of the same. In the end, the storm flooded many other homes deep into the interior and only time would prove some to be uninhabitable. Those that survived the flooding were left with one hell of a mess.

When she came to the intersection to cross Highway 71, she had to wait. A long convoy of power utility trucks rolled into town and turned left in front of her, heading to the elementary and high school. As far as she could see, the bucket trucks kept coming. They were from all over the South and beyond. As she watched the calvary roll into town, the weight of what she and her neighbors were about to face pressed her down into the seat. She sobbed uncontrollably. The clean-up had begun.

Nothing marks a weather-stricken hurricane region like the ubiquitous blue tarps. Hurricane Michael was no different. If anything, it was worse. Way worse. The blue canopy that covered the storm's path stretched for hundreds of miles, well into Georgia. If you still had a roof, chances are it was destined for a tarp.

Like nothing else, natural disasters bring out the very best in people. The charitable urge to help a fellow neighbor is infectious. But when all your fellow neighbors have problems of their own, there is little help that they can spare. Everyone is left to their own devices. One of Charlene's biggest challenges was being alone. Yes, being a female didn't help, but Charlene's a strong southern woman, and she never once saw that as an issue.

She knew the roof would need a proper repair. Thankfully, there was no rain in the immediate forecast, but what she needed most was a patch, and a good one. And it came through another answered prayer. It wasn't an elaborate prayer, but more of a quiet request for Divine intervention. Sometimes He likes those prayers the best.

The next morning, Charlene was on the grounds cleaning up limbs and blown debris from God knows where. As she dragged palm fronds to a pile on the street, a pickup truck pulling a long, covered trailer stopped in from of the house. The driver hoped out.

"Morning, Ma'am. My name is Charles Reilly, like Charles Nelson Reilly, but I'm not nearly as funny. Not at all."

That put a much-needed smile on her face.

"Anyway, me and the boys here came down from Dothan to lend a hand where it is needed..."

As he spoke, she bent over to look in the truck at the smiling faces and waves.

"...we got chainsaws, tools, ladders, water..."

She listened to the list of supplies and things that these lovely men could do to assist. Then she heard him say something that piqued her interest.

"...we even have tarps."

Charlene snapped to attention. "You have a tarp?"

"Yes, Ma'am. We have plenty of tarps. Do you need one?"

Charlene covered her mouth with the fingers of one hand, then used the same to pull a tear from her cheek. The words didn't come, so she nodded.

That put a big smile on Charles's face. "Show me."

"Follow me."

As he followed her, he turned toward the truck. "Get out boys. Grab the ladder, we got tarp work."

When Charlene heard the truck doors slam, she stopped and turned around. "How much is this going to cost? I don't have a lot of money."

Charles smiled. "All we ask is that you join us for a quick prayer before we start and another one before we leave."

Charlene heard the guys getting stuff out of the back of the trailer. That's when she saw what was printed on the side: The Dothan Baptist Disaster Recovery Team. She cried again, and said, "I'm a Methodist, just so you know."

Charles smiled and said, "Well, none of us are perfect."

Charlene laughed through her tears. "You, Mr. Charles, are funnier than you think."

As they walked to inspect the damage, she said, "Could I ask you another question?"

"Anything."

"By any chance... is it possible you have something that... well... isn't blue?"

Mr. Reilly stopped and caught her smile.

Then Charlene said, "Jus' say'n."

26

I Got You

M r. Reilly and his crew were a blessing, but they were only a small example of the outpouring of faith-based organizations that showed up to help the community. Church organizations, big and small, such as the one from Dothan, showed up from all over the South and came to assist, expecting nothing in return. Some only had chainsaws, others helped with yard cleanup, some brought water, and some brought generators. Some showed up every day to provide hot meals to hungry and exhausted people. They came to do the Lord's work and there was plenty to do.

It isn't a competition, but there isn't a group better equipped or prepared to help those in need than Samaritan's Purse out of North Carolina. Operating from their tractor-trailer, they systematically covered the entire area, going from household to household to assess and triage the needs of others. Once the list was created, a small army set out every day to do what nobody else was capable of. Starting with the most critical needs, they did everything from ripping out walls and tearing up floors to general repairs.

All the organizations that came to help were a blessing. And while some of those angels could only stay for a few days or weeks, Samaritan's Purse stayed for months, nearly six months.

It was nothing short of amazing.

In all fairness, it would be irresponsible to omit the response from the Federal Government. FEMA was on station from day one providing basic needs: ice, water, meals ready to eat, better known as MREs. Then they transitioned into providing more sustainable assistance, such as temporary housing, for those that lost it all.

And of course, there were the leeches, the scoundrels that came in looking to profit off the misery of others. As access to the war zone eased, in came the bastards. We won't give them much attention here, just know He has a special place in mind for them.

Those hard-hat angels from the power companies performed one of the most amazing feats. The damage to the electrical grid was so significant, they replaced the whole thing with the latest technology and systems, and they did it in record time. In Port St. Joe, you couldn't look down any street and not see seven or eight trucks working the lines.

It is sad, but much of that miracle came off the back of their neighbors to the west. The damage to Mexico Beach had been so devastating, the clean-up to allow trucks in took much longer. Plus, very little of the existing infrastructure remained, so it was a system in need of a complete rebuild. So, for the first several weeks after the storm, utility resources meant for Mexico Beach remained in St. Joe.

A few days after the storm, the word got out that the CVS was operating on generators and could take credit and debit cards. A corporate disaster team from other CVSs came in to run the store while their normal employees could cope with their own storm damage. Another blessing.

Charlene went to gather some supplies. It wasn't a lot, just a few items to get her through the next few days. They had one register running, but the system wasn't firing on all cylinders. Transactions were slow to complete. The line was long, but everybody remained understanding and patient.

They scanned Charlene's items, and she swiped her card. She looked up at the man behind the counter and watched him frown and shake his head.

"Try it again," he said.

She did, and nothing happened.

Two seconds later, a guy came running up. "Charlie. The system is down again. We're working on getting the connection back."

"Thanks, Stanley." Then he addressed the line. "Sorry folks. Looks like the system is down right now. We won't be able to take cards. Cash only."

Charlene exhaled in defeat. She looked at the total. Forty-two dollars and seventeen cents. She opened her purse, went through her cash, and looked at the man behind the counter. "I'm sixteen dollars short. I'll need to put some of this back."

Charlie frowned. "I'm sorry, lady."

"It's okay. It's not your fault."

From behind her, somebody said, "No. It isn't okay. I got you."

Charlene turned around. A utility lineman from Hart County stood smiling.

"No, sir. You don't need to do that. I'll be fine."

"Forget it. I got you."

"Really... You don't..."

"You're right. I don't, but I will." He reached over to the man behind the counter with several bills. "Here. This should cover it."

"Thank you," said Charlene. "You didn't..."

The man smiled. "But I just did. Now go on. You're holding up the line."

She gathered her things and headed toward the door. When the automatic doors flew open and the October heat hit her in the face, she stopped and turned around to wait. The man walked her way, still smiling.

He was going to walk past her, but she shifted her stance to block his way. He stopped.

"May I ask you a question?"

He said nothing.

"Where are you staying?"

"We're sleeping in the back of a tractor-trailer. There are two more with me."

Charlene thought long and hard, then said, "I have a small two-bedroom apartment above where I live. If you would like to come look at it, you and your guys could stay there."

"Really? Are you sure?"

"Sir, you just paid for my food. I can't have you sleeping in some old hot and dirty truck. I can't take everybody, but... Would you like to see it?"

"Yes, ma'am. I think I would."

He followed her to the unit, and it was perfect. He and his crew would have proper beds to sleep on. It was the last thing he expected. "Now... are you sure about this?"

"I'm sure I wish I could put every one of y'all up, but I can't. I can help y'all, though."

"Miss... You really don't..."

Charlene turned her head and threw up her hand. The roles had been reversed. "I got you."

It just goes to show how God works his grace and blessings by putting the right person into the lives of others.

27

WEEKS LATER

They quickly fell into a nice routine. While Charlene's little band of linemen worked their incredibly long hours, she returned to the boutique to sort things out and help get the shop into a position to reopen in the coming weeks. Not that there would be a huge demand for high-end clothing and accessories that soon after the storm. But just getting any of the stores back open, as soon as possible, helped with the illusion that things were getting back to normal. When, in reality, they weren't.

They would all pool their money, and Charlene would drive to Tallahassee to pick up provisions. And when her angel crew returned home from work each night, they were thankful for the cold showers and the hot meals she would cook for them. It was about as normal an existence as anyone could hope for, given the circumstances. They made the best of what they had.

They were getting close, but they had not yet restored power at Charlene's. That meant the daily drives to the elementary school for ice would continue.

Every day, as she drove through town, the piles and piles of debris continued to grow out by the street. Much of it came from the demolition efforts to tear out walls and wet insulation before mold could set in. Much of it was flooring. But even more heartbreaking were the pieces of destroyed memories that were mixed in. You can always replace floors, walls, and furniture. Other things, not so much. It was sobering.

Yes, she and the guys were making the best out of what they had. Others had to make the best out of a lot less. And in the coming days, when they restored her power, she was thankful that she wouldn't have to see that part of town every day. But that didn't stop the mounds from growing.

The end of October closed in fast and much had been accomplished. Many other shops and businesses in town had reopened. One of which was The Laundry Basket. Clothes had piled up over time, so Charlene took several loads to get washed, which included some of the crew's clothes. As she was sorting out colors and checking pockets, she came across a piece of paper. Written across the front was a phone number and a name: Bill Salisbury. It dawned on her. She'd been so busy since getting into town that she had almost forgotten about the nice British man that welcomed her and Zoey aboard his boat. To make matters worse, she felt any appreciation she displayed toward him had been inadequate. After all, because of him, she did not have to endure a painfully uncomfortable night in her car.

I wonder what happened to him; she thought.

She looked at the number and grabbed her phone. There wasn't a cell signal, but there would be one later. One carrier had brought in a mobile tower and turned it from six to nine in the evening. She stuffed the paper back in her pocket and loaded a machine.

28

SHALIMAR, FLORIDA

B ill sat on the back of *Think or Swim*, going over reports to prepare for a conference call that was scheduled for later that night with the office in India. He drank a Strongbow and looked out over the water. He had made it as far as Two Georges Marina in Shalimar, just outside Fort Walton Beach. Life was normal. Boats came and went. There was no drama, no crisis, and certainly no hurricane aftermath. Reminders of Hurricane Michael were long gone. The shock and devastation of the largest storm to hit the Panhandle had fallen off the news cycle. And certainly, the radar of most of the nation. For most, it was life as usual.

It was a little after six when his phone rang. He saw the name on the screen. She, too, had given him her number.

He answered. "Hello."

She smiled at his accent. "It's me, Bill. Charlene. Do you remember me?"

The sound of her southern drawl made him smile too. "Ah, yes. If I remember correctly, you were the axe-murdering bonnie lass I allowed to stay on my boat. Lucky for me, I escaped and locked myself away in the cabin."

"Oh, hush!"

They spent the next few minutes getting caught up, even

though they had only a brief history. She again expressed her deep thanks for the way he helped her that night.

"It was nothing," said Bill. "Just the right thing to do. I wouldn't have slept had I left you out there."

"Well, if you are ever over this way, I'd love to buy you a drink or dinner or something."

"That would be nice. In fact, I'll be over there in a couple of days. I need to check on my plane. It is over at Apalachicola, and I haven't seen it since the storm. They tell me it is fine, but until I see it for myself, I can't be sure."

This was the first mention of a plane, and it caused a slight rise of the eyebrows.

"We could meet then. Do you mind if I bring Danny? You remember Danny, right? He's the other bloke that caught us drinking wine and eating cheese."

"Oh, yes. That would be fine."

***

The three of them ended up eating at Provisions, one of St. Joe's better restaurants. They sat and drank and ate and talked and laughed and talked some more. They were so deep into conversation that the time had escaped them. Everyone else had left, the kitchen had closed, and the wait staff patiently stood off in the wings, never once hinting that it was time to go home.

"Oh, my God," said Charlene. "Look at the time." She looked around and found a waiter. "We are so sorry. This is embarrassing."

They felt bad about keeping the place open, but not for long. When they walked out onto the street, Reid Avenue was a ghost town. Bill walked Charlene to her car. Halfway there, he stopped. She stopped and turned, and he gave her a little kiss on the lips.

Ooooo, she thought, *that was kinda nice.*

They stood by the curb. She had a big smile on her face, so he was pretty sure he wasn't going to get slapped. Then he said, "If you would like, Charlene, please come see me in Shalimar. We could go out to dinner and maybe take in a movie or something."

"That would be nice. Sounds fun."

"How does Saturday at noon sound? You could come early. We'll make a whole day of it. The boat is at Two Georges Marina. Do you know where that is?"

"No. But I'll find it."

Bill smiled and opened her door for her. She got in, and before he closed the door, said, "See you then."

***

It was a long drive to Shalimar. Mexico Beach was still closed to anything but property owners and essential personnel, so Charlene had to detour around through Wewa and take Highway 22 into Panama City. It took over three hours to drive there, but Charlene arrived around a little after eleven in the morning.

Bill worked away on his laptop from the back of the boat. When he saw her walking down the dock, he looked at his watch. He closed the lid and met her on the dock.

"Hello, Charlene. Welcome. Welcome. I wasn't expecting you for another hour, so the place may be a bit in shambles."

Charlene bit at a knuckle, then, with a mischievous grin,

said, "I *might* have forgotten you were on Central Time. Did I catch you at a bad time?"

He realized she had gotten there early on purpose, and it made him happy. "No. Not at all. Make yourself at home. I think you know your way around, or at least you should. I just have a few things to finish up for work." He saw a hint of disappointment on her face, so he said, "Oh, screw it. It can wait."

They had a great day. They lounged around and talked the day away, much as they did while at dinner just a few days prior. There was no agenda, no schedule, no plan. They just hung out. The TV came on, but this time it was Bill's idea to watch music videos, or at least have them playing in the background. They later left for a bite to eat. Bill took her to a nice restaurant and the meal and company were exceptional. While having dinner, they both concluded, without telling the other, that they liked one another. For now, it would be their little secret to keep from the other. They were both thinking, *Let's see how things work out.*

After dinner, Charlene made the long ride back to St. Joe. Bill once again offered the settee in the salon, but she graciously refused and left for her car after a nice, long kiss. He tried to walk her to the car, but she declined. "I'll be fine. Talk to you soon?"

"I hope so."

The trip to Shalimar was a much-needed distraction, but the closer she got to home, the more frequent the reminders of Michael appeared. And as she pulled into town, a part of her just wanted to turn around. But that wouldn't have been right. She was in a special position. Having not suffered as much as others, she often struggled from a bit of survivor's guilt. So, giving back in little ways helped to ease that unwarranted anxiety. And she knew the best way she could help was through the stomach. Cooking was her thing.

The next morning, she slept in. That is until a gentle knocking at the door brought her around. It was her utility angels. All three stood holding their hard hats.

"Are y'all off to work?" she asked, rubbing her eyes.

"Sorry to wake you, and yes. Sort of, but we didn't want to leave without saying goodbye."

She straightened up. "I don't understand."

"They are moving us to work on the Mexico Beach rebuild. We found out yesterday, but you weren't around."

"Oh, my. So, you are leaving, leaving."

"Yes, we'll need to stay closer to the project. So... Well, anyway... we just wanted to say thanks. We sure are grateful for all you have done for us. We won't forget it."

She teared up. "I think you did more for me than you think. You guys gave me purpose and something to look forward to at the end of each day. Are you sure you can't just drive back and forth? You're welcome, you know."

"Yes, we know, but no. We'll need to stay close."

They all hugged out in the drive to say their goodbyes. When they were done, Charlene wiped her tears and slapped one of them on the arm. "Now you guys go over there and pay for some old, lonely gal's groceries and you might get lucky again."

They all laughed. The guys left. And she was alone, again.

29

THE FRIENDSGIVING

A week later, Charlene made a list of all the items she would need for an epic Thanksgiving meal. Madelyn, Spencer, and Ophelia, the granddaughter, came down from Tennessee. And the goal was to have enough food to feed anybody that wanted to eat. She put the word out to her neighbors and the invite spread. She didn't call it Thanksgiving, though. It was Friendsgiving.

As she jotted on her list, her phone dinged with a text notification. It was just a picture taken from the air. Where there weren't fluffy clouds, farm fields filled the background. Charlene knew Bill had gone to Ohio for a few days to work, so this must have been his way of letting her know he was headed back. She typed.

What are you doing for Thanksgiving?

I have nothing planned.

Come here and join our Friendsgiving. We have a spare cottage on the property, and you can stay the night and not have to drive back.

Splendid.

Bring Danny if he would like to come.

He's seeing a new girl from the homeland. May she come?

The more the merrier. Anybody can come. It's all about

friends.

The first-ever Friendsgiving was a hit. People showed up. Some brought a dish to share, and some just brought their appetites, which was fine. There was plenty of food. It was a feast.

There was no table to sit around, so they made a big circle with plastic chairs. Some of the faces were familiar, some were not. Charlene was thrilled with the outcome. Once everybody finished, they sat in the circle and told storm stories.

During the conversations, things took an odd and weird turn.

Danny had already introduced his new friend, Mandy, to Bill the week before. She was quite attractive and from Peterborough, an eastern city known for its wild party lifestyle. Well, Mandy proved to live up to her region's reputation. She had already taken a shine and fancy to Bill the week before and made sure that she sat next to him in the circle. As Bill and Charlene had their hands on each other's thighs, Mandy made the bold move of placing her hand on Bill's other inner thigh. Bill ignored it, and Charlene did the same. To reward her, he leaned over and kissed Charlene on the cheek, and gave her a wink. But, from the other side of the circle, Madelyn and Spencer were an audience to the activity. Madelyn looked at her mom and Charlene returned a quirky smile. Madelyn looked at Spencer and whispered, "That's just weird as shit." Then she looked at Mandy. "Hey, you!"

Everybody turned to look at Madelyn. Mandy now knew she was being addressed and Charlene's eyes almost bugged out her head. She turned to Bill and said, "Uh, oh."

Then Madelyn curled one side of her upper lip and said, "What exactly in the fuck do you think you are doing?"

Spencer thought, *Saw that coming.* Before she could say

anything else, he tried to defuse the situation. "What is that? Like some British thing?"

Everybody laughed but Madelyn and Mandy.

"Well," said Madelyn, never taking her eyes off Mandy, "if she doesn't move her damn hand, she just might learn a thing or two about a South Georgia thing."

Bill looked at Charlene. "You're right. She holds nothing back, does she?"

"I know. She gets it from her damn daddy."

They laughed and stood to go get more pie.

Later that evening, after the crowd had dispersed and the cleanup was done, Bill and Charlene sat in the cozy living room of the small cottage he was staying in.

"Did you enjoy yourself today?" she asked.

"I had a wonderful time. And the food was delicious. I just wish..." He went silent for a while, and Charlene waited.

"I just wish there was someplace over here to keep the boat. I really don't like it over at Shalimar. It is way too touristy. I just don't like it."

"You could go to Scipio Creek."

"Where?"

"Scipio Creek. In Apalachicola."

"There isn't a proper marina in Apalachicola, is there?" He pulled out his phone and pulled up his Snag-A-Slip app and showed it to Charlene. "See. There is nothing on the map to list an adequate marina."

"Well, I don't know about that app. Hell, the whole town of Apalach is lucky to be listed on a map. It is the most unassuming town in the world. Have you even been there?"

"No. Never been closer than the airport, and I've had no reason to go into town."

"If I ask you to run by and check on it the next time you go to your plane, will that be reason enough?"

"I promise."

"Thank you. Well, it's getting late. I better go."

"Thank you, again, for asking me to come. I had a delightful time."

Charlene moved in closer. "You are quite welcome."

Next door on the porch, Madelyn and Spencer sat in the cool evening breeze. Enjoying the night. Spencer had his head back, his hands on his belly, and his eyes closed until he felt the smack on his arm. "What the hell?"

"Look, dammit," said Madelyn, pointing to the silhouette on the window shade. "Momma is kissing that man. Damn, she is acting like a teenager."

Spencer chuckled, "Well... it seems she likes the British thing, too."

30

BOOBIES AND THE BRIDGE

Two weeks later, Charlene was refolding a bunch of clothes that snowbird tourists from New Jersey had rifled through. Charlene watched from behind the counter as they picked up almost every shirt or dress, waved it free of its folds and held it up against their torso. "How does this one look, Stella?"

The woman named Stella waved her hand in disgust. "Oh, dear. I wouldn't be caught dead in that dreadful thing. But Ava, oh! How does this look?"

"Oh, girl. I like it. The color is good on you."

Stella threw it back down on the table. "I knew you would say that. Have you no taste, Ava? It is perfectly an abomination."

It went on like that for twenty minutes, and the longer they stayed, the more the store became disarrayed. But after Stella announced her last, "Just ghastly!" they left buying nothing.

Charlene mumbled to herself. "Oh, Ava. Dreadful. Horrid. You can't be serious. Uggg!" Then her phone dinged. It was a text message from Bill. Another picture without description. It was a boat dock next to brown water.

She responded. *Okay, you got me. What is it?*

My new home.

Charlene scrunched her nose. Then another message came through.

At Scipio Creek in Apalach

Charlene squealed and called him immediately.

"So, you checked it out, huh?"

"I'm here now with Danny. I love it. It is perfect. Quiet. Not crowded. And I have my own alligator."

"An alligator?"

"Yes, he's floating in my slip now. The old boy will have to move, though."

"So, you're going to get it?"

"Already have. Paid for a full year."

"That's so exciting. When?"

"Sometime next week, when my Shalimar slip comes due."

"I'm so excited."

"Me too."

***

Sunday, December 16, 2018, was warmer than usual. Afternoon temps reached into the low to mid-seventies, a perfect day to cruise to Apalachicola and tie up at Scipio Creek Marina. What made the day seem even nicer was the break it gave to the copious amounts of rain they had received over the past weeks. It was good to see blue skies again.

As *Think or Swim* buzzed along the ICW and approached the White City Bridge, Bill could see somebody standing on the dock. The closer he got to White City, the more he was convinced. It was Charlene, and she had her thumb stuck out looking to hitch a ride.

He didn't realize she would be there, but he had been texting his progress, so it didn't surprise him to find her waiting. It made him glad. He slowed way down and pulled closer to the dock. From the flying bridge, he yelled, "Where to, young lady?"

"Scipio Creek!" she yelled.

"Well, my goodness. What a coincidence. Get ready to grab a line."

After securing the boat, he jumped down to the dock and kissed her. "How long have you been waiting?"

"I don't know. Forty-five minutes or so."

"I'm glad you came. Hop aboard and let's get a move on."

It was a pleasurable, lazy passage through the ICW and across the wide Lake Wimico. But things picked up once they reached the pin hook, that section where the Apalachicola River dumps into the ICW. They would be in Apalach sooner than they thought. The boat enjoyed a faster-than-normal ride. The flood waters from the Apalachicola River only added to the already swift current. *Think or Swim* had rarely seen such speeds, doing nine knots over the ground. She now zipped along at a healthy clip.

Bill had the boat on autopilot and controlled the helm from his iPad as he and Charlene sat on the bow. They did more kissing and fooling around than paying attention to *Think and Swim* and her progress.

Ahead waited the old swing bridge train trestle that served the Apalachicola Northern Railroad. For decades, the tracks transported paper mill goods from Port St. Joe to destinations north toward Georgia. Once the paper mill closed, it wasn't long before the swing-bridge was left open to boat traffic for good. It hasn't been used since and has rusted itself in place.

Unbeknownst to either Bill or Charlene, the rushing current had both passages through the trestle in aquatic turmoil. The rushing waters cutting through the support pilings had the passage in a swirling mess. Not good for a boat with very limited propulsion power. Not to mention, Bill and Charlene were playing kissy face.

Damn kids. I had to lean into Charlene's ear and whisper, "Look up, Charlie."

"Huh?" she said, looking around. Then she saw it. "Bill." He kept wanting to kiss. She had to pull her head back, away from his leaning lips. "Bill! Look. We are going to hit the bridge."

Bill gave it a quick assessment. "No. She will be fine. She'll turn."

They went back to kissing, but Charlene kept one eye on the bridge. "Bill! I'm telling you. We're gonna hit that bridge."

Bill looked up. Then grabbed his iPad controller, only to see that he lost his connection with the autopilot. "Oh, shit!" He scrambled to the helm and did his best to maneuver the boat away from the piling, but... "Hold on, Charlene! Hold on!"

Seconds later. *CRRRUUUUUNNNNCH!*

It was a sickening sound. One of the massive rusty bolts protruding from a piling breeched *Think or Swim's* topsides and ripped a massive hole along the side. Once the boat broke free, Bill got it back on course and ran down to look over the side. What he saw made him cringe, but it was above the waterline, so they weren't sinking. He looked up to find Charlene standing with her hands on her hips. They were about to have their first argument. Sort of. "Are you okay?"

"I am fine. I told *you* we were going to hit that bridge, but you wouldn't listen."

"This is all your bloody fault."

"My fault? The hell you say."

"Yes. You told me a bit too late; wouldn't you say?"

"Late?" Now her arms were crossed. "You were the one that

said, 'She will be fine. She'll turn.'"

"But... you were distracting me!"

She said nothing.

"With your tits!"

They both stood looking at each other in silence. Then they both broke out in laughter. When they caught their breath, Bill said, "Go on now. Go below and take your boobies with you. I need to concentrate."

She did as she was told, but not before pulling down on her shirt to give him one last tease.

"Go on now! I mean it."

They've been laughing ever since.

31

BEEEEL!... FROM NORTH GEORGIA

From that dreadful day after Michael, when he invited Charlene and Zoey onto the boat, it only took a bit over nine weeks for them to become inseparable. Since the day they delivered a battered and holey *Think or Swim* to Apalachicola, you rarely saw one without the other. When he wasn't staying with her in St. Joe, she was on the boat. When he had international travel lined up for pleasure or business, she sat next to him on the plane. It wasn't just a matter of them enjoying each other's company. They sincerely couldn't bear the thought of being away from each other. It was more than *meant to be*. It was a *match made from heaven*. And I mean that... *literally*. Ha!

Bill not only gained a fantastic lady, but she put a pot load of new friends in his midst. New friends, who he embraced and has become quite fond of. Sure, he has Danny, who remains his best mate. Bill will never know that it was *I* that caused him to stop that first time in White City. And for sure, just to clear the air, I had *nothing to do* with his experiment with Tinder. Although it seemed to play out well enough within the plan. Thanks, New Delhi Jerry, wherever you are.

But the story doesn't really end here. Although they were making a life for themselves, it didn't quite seem complete.

Once, while Charlene was working at the boutique, Bill and Danny enjoyed a few Strongbows on the back of the boat. Looking over Scipio Creek, Danny said, "You really fancy this one, don't you?"

"I can't stop thinking of her, Danny. It's been over six months now, and it feels as new as it did way back then."

"When did you know she was the lucky one?"

"I'm the lucky one, mate. But... if I had to nail down a time. It must be the morning after our Friendsgiving. I was packing to leave, and she came over to the cottage to say goodbye." Bill stopped to replay the moment.

"And?"

"She hadn't even said a word. She just smiled and looked at me. There was something about her eyes. Yes, it was those eyes. They were the most kind and sincere eyes I had ever seen. There was a sparkle that drilled a hole straight through me. I had never seen eyes like that before, and I couldn't take my eyes off them. Even after I left for Shalimar, I could stop thinking about them. It was then that I thought, *Shit. Something good is going on here.* Next thing I know, a few weeks later, we were kissing on the bow of the boat. She had her boobies right there, and we crashed the boat. I think that sealed the deal."

Danny said nothing and let Bill keep talking.

"If she'll marry me, will you be my best man?"

"You know I will mate."

In the coming days, Bill thought long and hard about how he would ask her. He knew he wanted to surprise her, but how? When he let her sisters and daughter in on his intentions, they were thrilled. But it was Madelyn that said, "Momma is a southern girl. You might not understand, but you need to make it as redneck as possible. Have a party, invite all her friends, and propose to her in front of them."

"Redneck, you say. Charlene doesn't seem like much of a redneck."

"Trust me, Bill. You are right. Momma is pretty sophisticated, but you can't take the country out of the girl. For example, nothing can be more redneck than proposing to her from the bed of an old, beat-up pickup truck."

"But I don't have an old pickup truck."

"Shit, Bill... do I have to spell it out for you? Get one!"

That set things in motion.

At the recommendation of her sisters, Bill met with Mike Baxter of Baxter's Jewelry in Donalson, GA. Mike was the family jeweler and should be included in designing a ring for Charlene. Mike was thrilled and knew exactly how to make it all special.

It was September, and with the help of Charlene's St. Joe girlfriends, they planned a beach party. Which wasn't really anything special. It wasn't anything out of the ordinary to gather several trucks on the beach and enjoy beers and hot dogs on the grill. To Charlene, it was just another Forgotten Coast gathering.

It wasn't an old pickup that Bill and Charlene showed up in. Bill bought a new GMC Sierra, but it was a truck. It would have to do.

The day was like any other, but her suspicions were heightened once her daughter, granddaughter, and sisters showed up as a surprise. Then, when Mike Baxter arrived, she gasped. It was time.

Everybody gathered around, and Bill pulled Charlene up in the truck bed. He did his best to be as redneck as possible, but that is a tall task for a British gentleman. He did a fine job and even took on a Southern persona. When folks ask him where he is from, he puts on his best Southern accent and says, "I'm

Beeel, from North Georgia." He even got the tag for his truck to say, Beeel.

In the end, it was beautiful, and they shed many tears. And of course, she said, "Yes."

32

COVID AND QUARANTINE

The plan was for a big beach wedding in the coming spring. Details were being discussed; some were complete. Things moved along well, and the closer they came to New Year's Day, the more excited they got. That celebration came and went with elevated fanfare in anticipation of what their future held.

Life was grand. Bill's business continued to grow at a healthy clip around the globe. And while Bill had already experienced the American Dream of success, now he had somebody to share it with. And while that would never change, other things did.

On January 9, 2020, the World Health Organization announced a mysterious corona related virus breakout in Wuhan, China. While reported in the news, it drew little attention from the American public, but the Center for Disease Control in Atlanta watched it closely. Once fresh cases were confirmed in Thailand and Japan, the CDC began screening at the three major airports that received flights from Wuhan. The very next day, the first confirmed case of what had been declared Covid-19 had reached the United States. A man in the state of Washington had brought the virus home after a recent visit to Wuhan. On the same day, Chinese scientists confirmed human-to-human transmission. Two days later, the entire region of Wuhan was placed under a mandatory quarantine, and surrounding cities were placed under arduous travel restrictions, placing over eighteen million people in lockdown. The virus gained much more attention from the media and public.

Cases were popping up across the nation, and on the first of March, Florida discovered its first two confirmed cases in Manatee and Hillsborough counties. Evidence continued to show that the virus was not just casually contagious, but extremely contagious.

In the coming weeks, cases were developing rapidly, and on March 21, 2020, the entire State of California was placed on a mandatory stay-at-home order. The country was slowly shutting down. Florida would soon follow suit with restrictions to activities not deemed essential.

With valid concerns about Charlene's past medical history, she and Bill went into their own voluntary quarantine. The rest of their 2020 was spent mostly in isolation, and their plans for a joyous wedding in the spring came to a sad halt.

In the early days of Covid-19, little was known about how it would affect the general population, which brought about aggressive measures to contain the spread. The economic impact was devastating to the country, and as time passed, it became clearer who was the most vulnerable; the elderly, those with certain medical conditions, and weakened immunities.

With these additional facts established, Governor DeSantis of Florida shifted the state's response to a more targeted approach. He reopened the state's economic machine and focused on protecting the most vulnerable. In an announcement, he stated: "We're not shutting down, we're gonna go forward, we're gonna continue to protect the most vulnerable... particularly when you have a virus that disproportionately impacts one segment of society, to suppress a lot of working-age people at this point I don't think would likely be very effective."

This novel approach opened the possibility that wedding plans could resume, but Bill and Charlene stayed the course. They remained in quarantine and stayed vigilant. Protecting Charlene was Bill's top priority, but at least they felt they could again entertain what new wedding plans might look like. That was encouraging.

It was in October, the second anniversary of Hurricane Michael had come and gone. Progress was being made in St. Joe. Much of it, though, was from the altered landscape. The demolitions and cleanup along Highway 98 and many of the residential blocks behind it left empty lots where small family homes once stood. As a member of a community, it's difficult to understand just how much one relies on little landmarks for navigation until those little reminders are gone. The mind wants to see that little yellow corner house on Monument Avenue before turning onto Thirteenth. It expects to see those bayside homes on Highway 98 that subliminally say, "Fourteenth Street is coming up," not flat empty parcels with For Sale signs. It would take a while before the mind is retrained and the turns are not missed.

Charlene and Bill sat on the back of the boat, enjoying wine, a cool evening, and the sounds of the creek and marsh. Bill got up to put on some music, and Charlene browsed through her missed Facebook memories. When Bill returned, he found her crying with a hand over her mouth.

"My God, Charlene? What has got you in such a state?"

She grinned and held up her phone. He took it and looked at the picture. "What is this about?"

"Bill. That is the last sunset picture I took before the hurricane. It was just Sadie and me."

"Okay?"

"Look at the picture, Bill. Your boat is there in its slip. I took that picture just days before we met."

"That is something, isn't it? What a crazy coincidence."

"I don't think it's crazy. I think it is divine."

Bill took his seat, and the quiet resumed for a period, then Charlene said, "Let's just elope. I'll call Sadie and you call Danny to stand for us."

"Charlene. You know that isn't what you want."

"I just want you as my husband. I'm sick of all this mess. Covid, isolation, everything. If we just went and got married, maybe all this might feel more normal."

Bill said nothing, but he smiled and reached over to take her hand.

"What do you say?"

"I say I want you as my wife, too. And..."

"And what?"

"I've been thinking. I'm still not comfortable with a big wedding, but what if we move our quarantine to a beach house and invite all your core girlfriend besties and their husbands? We will keep it small and intimate. No outsiders."

Charlene's eyes flashed with excitement. "Do you mean it?"

"I wouldn't have mentioned it if I didn't."

"We'll need to find a minister and a photographer that will come out."

"No. No outsiders," he said. "We'll need to keep it an inside job. Didn't you say that Scott, Donna's husband, is a photographer?"

"He is."

"Okay, problem solved, if he'll do it."

"I'm sure he will, but we'll need a minister."

"I've been thinking and looking into that, too. Somebody can get ordained from one of those online minister websites. It's easy and legal."

"Really? But who?"

Their minds wandered for a few moments. Then, they looked at each other and said, "Aubrey!"

"Have you given any thought about who will give you away?" asked Bill.

"It has to be John, Peyton's husband. He's the closest thing to blood family I have. I hope he's up to it. The cancer has been a struggle."

"If I had to guess, he wouldn't miss it for the anything."

Charlene put her wine down, got up, jumped into his lap, spilled his wine, wrapped her arms around him, and said, "I love you."

33

LETTING GO

B ill found a beach house big enough to accommodate everyone. He booked it for the entire week after New Year's Day. The plan was for everyone to converge on the property on the day of check-in, fully provision it with food and drink for the week and remain on station all week long. When the time felt right, a simple, personalized ceremony would be held down by the water.

Slowly, the gang showed up. Lydia and her husband, the other Danny, Aubrey and Alan, Donna and Scott, with his camera at the ready, Cloe and Joe, and, of course, Sadie. It was all perfect, except for one thing. There was a vast hole in the group. Just weeks before, Sadie's husband Beau took unexpectantly ill and passed away. It was devastating for them all. Understandably, Sadie struggled, but continued with the plan. Having her St. Joe girls surrounding her and sharing their love provided great relief and therapy.

In the days leading up to the wedding, the weather couldn't have been more perfect. Mild temperatures made for wonderful, relaxing days on the beach, complete with fishing lines cast out into the surf by Aubrey's husband, Alan. There was plenty to eat and drink. Every night was a party full of food, fun, beer, wine, and booze. YouTube videos of Joe

Bonamassa, Beth Hart, and the band JJ Grey & Mofro filled the space with music and dance. They ate a banquet every night. The memories mounted minute by minute and were all captured by the camera.

Then one night, Charlene made an announcement. "Tomorrow is the day, ladies."

The entire household squealed with excitement. And Lydia said, "Oh my God. We have to have a rehearsal." That brought on more squeals.

People should probably not do wedding rehearsals while under the influence of libations, but that's what they did. It was all goofy, fun, and totally ridiculous, to the point of absurdity. I'm not sure who said it, but someone tried to convince them to at least have one serious go at it. The girls all yelled, "NO!" So, if they accomplished one thing that night, it was rehearsing what would *not* happen the next day.

The excess from the night before delivered some foggy heads the next morning, but it did little to curb the excitement of what the afternoon would bring. During a light breakfast and mimosas, Bill's mate Danny arrived with the wedding cake. A 3-D replica of *Think or Swim* underneath the White City Bridge. It was certainly appropriate, and Charlene and the ladies loved it.

British Danny asked to excuse himself so he could change, then disappeared into a bathroom. Everyone went about their business around the big kitchen island, snacking on fruit and making more mimosas. When Charlene heard the bathroom door open, she gave a glance and became speechless. Danny emerged and walked into the kitchen and looked in the fridge. A few others noticed and their jaws dropped. Cloe mumbled, "Oh, dear." Finally, he closed the door and asked, "Bill, where are the ciders for crying out loud?"

Bill looked at his friend. "Danny. Good God, my boy, you're naked!"

"No, I'm not." Then he took off the wide-brimmed hat he wore and set it on the island. "Now, Now I'm naked. Now point me to the cider."

"Over there in the cooler, for crying out."

Everyone watched as Danny casually walked to the cooler, withdrew a Strongbow, and sauntered back to the bathroom. He stopped at the door, turned and said, "We're all naked, you know... underneath."

Everyone laughed, and he went in and closed the door.

Seconds later he reemerged, still without a stitch, and walked to the island. "Forgot my hat. Feel naked without it."

Then Lydia's Danny said, "He's a Naked Danny. That was cool as shit."

"Well," said Bill, "there will be no confusing the two of *you* anymore. Now we have a Danny and a Naked Danny."

Everyone laughed.

After breakfast, and Naked Danny put on some clothes, it was time to get serious about the day. The girls disappeared upstairs to help Charlene get ready. Lydia did her hair as the rest of the girls helped in the primping and the making of more mimosas.

Scott was the only guy allowed in, and that was only long enough to capture some memories. Charlene's gaggle of beauty consultants later ushered him out the door. When he got back downstairs, Bill asked, "How is it going up there?"

"Nobody is nervous. I can assure you of that."

As the magical hour approached, it was only Charlene and her maid of honor, Sadie, in the room. They waited patiently until everyone was ready down on the beach. At around four-thirty, Cloe came into the room. "We're ready if you are."

Charlene nodded her head and her mouth formed that huge signature smile. A couple of minutes later, she and Sadie came down the stairs. When she got to the bottom, I whispered in her ear. "You look beautiful, Charlie."

She stopped and looked around. She tilted her head to listen, but heard nothing more.

"What's the matter, Charlene?"

Charlene ignored her friend and looked toward the ceiling. "It's going to be alright, isn't it?"

Sadie said, "What are you talking about?"

"Yes, Charlie, it is." I leaned in and kissed her cheek. "Go on now, he's waiting."

She reached up, lightly touched where I had kissed her, then looked at her fingertips.

"Charlene... you're scaring me."

Charlene grabbed her friend's hand and said, "Come on. Everything is fine."

***

I decided on a bird's-eye view of the ceremony. I leaned up against the upstairs deck railing and watched. It was as beautiful and picturesque of a wedding scene as you could imagine. A simple but elegant wedding arbor had been set up by the surf. Aubrey stood with Bill and Naked Danny. The small assembly of family friends stood waiting. When Bill pointed at the house, everybody turned around. Sadie slowly made her way across the sand and took up her position. Then Charlene appeared and made her way toward the makeshift chapel. As she drew closer, a dear family friend joined her, John. For health reasons, he and his wife, Peyton, could not attend the weekly festivities. However, there was no way he was going to miss giving away the bride.

Bill looked at his best mate and whispered, "She is gorgeous."

"Yes, she is."

"I have you to blame for all this, you know?"

"What are friends for, mate?"

John and Charlene finished their walk down the salty aisle, and Aubrey said, "Who gives this woman to be married to this man?"

I watched as John put Charlene's hand into Bill's. And as the official ceremony began, another joined me. I turned to look at him. "Hey, you must be Beau. I heard you might be coming. I'm Michael but call me Mike."

"Glad to meet you. Wouldn't have missed it for anything."

I said nothing and gazed down at the proceedings.

"So, I understand your work here is almost done."

"Yeah. It took a while, but that seems to be the case." I looked at my new friend. "You have your work cut out for you."

"I know. She's taking it hard."

"It's early. She'll be fine. Just stay at it and help her along."

"Look," said Beau, pointing. "He's kissing the bride."

Cheers roared from down on the beach, followed by hugs and tears of joy.

As we watched from the balcony, Beau asked, "Hey, you wouldn't happen to have a cowbell, would you?"

When he turned to look at me... I was gone. He nodded his head a few times and turned his attention toward his beautiful, widowed wife. "Hang in there, Sadie. I love you."

The End!

Thank You!

If you enjoyed *Michael*, there are a few things you could do to thrill this author.

First, provide a short, honest review at Amazon. Those reviews mean so much more than you could imagine. It doesn't have to be long. We appreciate *star only* reviews too.

Second, please consider signing up for my monthly newsletter. There, you will gain some insight into my other books, especially the Nigel Logan Action Series and the knucklehead that created it. Oh... That would be me. PLUS! You can grab a **FREE** copy of *The Cuban,* a Nigel Logan novella I wrote just for you. And... If you join us, I will make you this one promise: *I will not fill your inbox with junk and SPAM.* Sign up at www.KirkJockell.com

And the third thing is, contact me. I love to hear from readers. Let me know what you thought of the book. It would make my day more than you can imagine.

Email: Kirk@KirkJockell.com
Facebook: www.facebook.com/KirkJockellAuthor
Website: www.KirkJockell.com
Book Bub: www.BookBub.com/Kirk S Jockell

ACKNOWLEDGEMENTS

Wow! This has been such a departure from writing my Nigel Logan books. As I mentioned on the copyright page, this is a work of faction. A fictional account of actual events that occurred after the storm. Of course, I took a few authors' liberties. How does it go?... Ah, yes... *Never let the truth stand in the way of a good story*. When I first caught wind of this tale, I knew I wanted to write it. I didn't know it would take me five years to get around to doing it. But... here it is.

Many already know who this story is about, but for this book, the couple wished to remain anonymous. And that is fine, but I can tell you this. I've never had more fun preparing to write anything. They were both so forthcoming during our recorded interviews. They shared many deep, personal details with me I knew would never make it into the story. Thank you both for putting your trust in me. I've had a blast going back to listen and laugh, and the fun part is, only they and I know what is fact and what is fiction, or some fun, strange combination of the two.

In addition, my most sincere appreciation goes out to so many people. None more so than my wonderful wife, Joy. She is my bride, my partner, my rock, and number one supporter. To do things without her would be impossible. Her love and encouragement are nothing short of amazing.

Then, there are those *real folks* that take the greatest risk of all and agree to make cameo appearances in these books. Folks like emergency room doctor Patrick Conrad and Paramedic Jonathan Cannon. These two exceptional medical professionals helped me keep the early scenes real. Plus, they kept me from looking like a total idiot. *Never a simple task.* Then, there's the Drunk Donkey of Mike's Weather Page. Thank you, Mike, for being a sport. There might not have been a story to tell had it not been for you.

Then, there are the folks that keep me from looking too stupid, which isn't easy. That I can promise. I brought Jan Wade and Tim "Coach" Slauter back into the saddle. And I'm glad I did. When reviewing their edits and suggestions, I shake my head and think, *You got to be kidding me?* Then there is the band of beta readers that helps me along. Thanks to all of you.

ABOUT THE AUTHOR

Kirk Jockell is an American writer and the creator of The Nigel Logan Action Series. He lives in Port St. Joe, Florida, where he patiently waits for his wife to retire, so she can join him for a simpler life down on The Forgotten Coast. Kirk is a sailor and an avid photographer of sailboats. He loves to fish, throw his cast net for mullet, listen to music (Pop Country doesn't count), play his guitar, and drive his Bronco on the beach. Kirk lives with his lovely wife Joy, a rescued bluetick coonhound named Nate (#98Nate), and a tuxedo cat named Mr. Hemingway.

OTHER WORKS BY KIRK S. JOCKELL

The Nigel Logan Action Series

The Tales from Stool 17 Trilogy
Finding Port St Joe (Book 1)
Trouble in Tate's Hell (Book 2)
Dark Days of Judgment (Book 3)
The Complete Trilogy (Box Set)

More Nigel Logan Books
Tough Enough (Prequel)
Tupelo Honey (Book 4)
Traffic (Book 5)
Tidewater Moon (Book 6)
Tormented (Book 7)
The Cuban (Novella)

Made in the USA
Columbia, SC
26 September 2023